THE
SECRET PRINCESS

THE
SECRET PRINCESS

BY

JESSICA HART

MILLS & BOON®

First published in Great Britain 2011
by Mills & Boon, an imprint of Harlequin (UK) Limited.
Large Print edition 2012
Harlequin (UK) Limited, Eton House,
18-24 Paradise Road, Richmond, Surrey TW9 1SR

© Jessica Hart 2011

ISBN: 978 0 263 22549 5

Harlequin (UK) policy is to use papers that are natural,
renewable and recyclable products and made from
wood grown in sustainable forests. The logging and
manufacturing process conform to the legal environmental
regulations of the country of origin.

Printed and bound in Great Britain
by CPI Antony Rowe, Chippenham, Wiltshire

For my dear niece, Suzy,
with love on her engagement.

CHAPTER ONE

WAVING her hands around her head in a futile attempt to bat the midges away, Lotty paused for breath at the crest of the track. Below her, an austere granite house was planted between a forbidding sweep of hillside and a loch so still it mirrored the clouds and the trees clustered along the water's edge.

Loch Mhoraigh House. It looked isolated and unfriendly and, according to all reports in the village, its owner was the same.

'He's the worst boss I've ever had.' Gary had been drowning his sorrows in the Mhoraigh Hotel bar all afternoon and his words were more than a little slurred. 'Not a smile, not a good morning, just straight to work! I told him if I'd wanted to work in a labour camp, I'd have signed up for one. It's not as if he's paying more than slave wages either, and he won't get anyone else. I told him what he could do with his job!'

'Quite right too.' Elsie, the barmaid, polished glasses vindictively and warned Lotty against making the trek out to Loch Mhoraigh House. 'We don't want Corran McKenna around here. The Mhoraigh estate should have gone to his brother, we all know that,' she said, hinting darkly at some family feud that Lotty didn't quite follow. 'Nobody from the village will work for him. You go on up to Fort William,' she told Lotty. 'You'll find a job there.'

But Lotty couldn't afford to go any further. Without her purse, she was penniless, and when you needed money, you got yourself a job, right?

Or so she had heard. The truth was that until an hour earlier, when she had realised that her purse was missing, Lotty had never in her life had to think about money at all.

Now she did.

It was Lotty's first challenge, and she was determined to rise to it. Her life was so luxurious, so protected. She understood why, of course, but it meant that she had never once been tested and, until you were, how did you know who you were and what you were made of? That was what these few short weeks were all about. Was there any more to Her Serene Highness Princess Charlotte of Montluce than the stylish clothes and the gracious smile that were all the rest of the world saw?

Lotty needed to know that more than anyone.

Here was her first chance to find out. When you didn't have any money, you had to earn some. Lotty set her slim shoulders and hoisted her rucksack onto her back. If everyone else could do it, she could too.

Three miles later, she was very tired, tormented by midges and, looking doubtfully down at the unwelcoming house, it occurred to Lotty, belatedly, that she could be making a terrible mistake. Loch Mhoraigh House was very remote, and Corran McKenna lived alone out here. Was it safe to knock on his door and ask if he could give her a job? What if Elsie had been right, and he was a man who couldn't be trusted? Elsie's dislike of him seemed to be based on the fact that he wasn't a real Scot, and she had implied that he had acquired the estate under false pretences.

It wasn't as if she didn't have a choice, Lotty knew that. One phone call, and a close protection team would be on its way within minutes. A helicopter would swoop down and scoop her up, and take her back to the palace in Montluce. There would be no midges there, no money worries, no need to put herself at risk. There would just be her grandmother to face, and the knowledge of her own uselessness. She would be the princess who ran away and couldn't last a week on her own.

Lotty grimaced at the thought of the humiliation. Three months, she had agreed with Philippe and Caro. Three months to disappear, to be anonymous, to see for herself what she was made of. She couldn't give up at the first difficulty, and slink home with her tail between her legs.

She was a princess of Montluce, Lotty reminded herself, and her chin lifted. Her family hadn't kept an iron grip on the country since the days of Charlemagne by giving up the moment the going got tough. She had been raised on the stories of the pride and courage that had kept Montluce independent for so long: Léopold Longsword, Princess Agathe who had been married off to a German prince nearly fifty years her senior in order to keep the succession safe, and of course the legendary Raoul the Wolf.

They had faced far greater challenges than Lotty. All she had to do was find herself a job.

Was she going to be the first of the Montvivennes to accept defeat?

No, Lotty vowed, she wasn't.

Lotty adjusted her rucksack more comfortably on her back, and set off down the rough track towards Loch Mhoraigh House.

The house loomed grey and massive as Lotty trudged wearily up to the front door. An air of neglect clung to everything. Weeds were growing in what had once been an impressive gravel drive and the windows were cold and cheerless. It was very quiet. No lights, no music, no sign of anyone living there. Only the crows wheeling above the Scots pines and the cry of some bird down by the loch.

Lotty hesitated, looking at the old-fashioned bell. What if Corran McKenna wasn't there? She wasn't sure her feet could take her back up that hill.

But what if he *was?* Lotty chewed her bottom lip uncertainly. She had never had to persuade anyone to give her a job before. She'd never really had to persuade anyone to do anything. Normally people fell over themselves to give her whatever she wanted. She led a charmed and privileged existence, Lotty knew, but it made it a lot harder to prove that she was a worthy successor to all those doughty ancestors who had fought and negotiated and bargained and married to keep Montluce free.

They wouldn't have been deterred by a simple no, and neither would she.

For these few weeks, she had abandoned her title and her household. There was no one to arrange things for her, no one to make sure she got exactly what she wanted.

She was going to have to do this for herself.

Taking a deep breath, Lotty pressed the bell.

She could hear it clanging inside the house somewhere. Immediately, a furious barking erupted. It sounded as if there was a whole pack of dogs in there, and instinctively Lotty took a step back. There was a sharp command and the dogs subsided, except for a high-pitched yapping that continued until it was suddenly stifled as a door was shut firmly on it.

A few moments later, the front door was jerked open.

A tall, tough-looking man, as forbidding as the hills behind the house, stood there. He was

younger than Lotty had expected, with dark, un-
compromising features and a stern mouth, and
his eyes were a pale, uncanny blue.

'Yes?'

'I've c-come about the job,' said Lotty, cursing
the stammer that still resurfaced at times when
she was nervous. Raoul the Wolf wouldn't have
stammered, she was sure.

His fierce brows snapped together. 'Job? What
job?'

'I heard in the hotel that you needed help restoring some cottages to let.'

'News travels fast...or did Gary stop at the bar
on his way back to Glasgow?' Corran added with
a sardonic look.

Lotty brushed at the midges that clustered at her
ears. Raoul the Wolf wouldn't have put up with
being left on the doorstep either, but she could
hardly insist that he invite her inside. She concentrated on sounding reasonable instead. 'He
said you didn't have anyone else and that you'd
be stuck without anyone to work for you.'

'And did he also say that it was the worst job
he'd ever done, not to mention being the worst
paid, and having the worst boss?'

'Something like that.'

'And yet you want to work for me?'

'I'm desperate,' said Lotty.

The pale eyes inspected her. Lotty had never been the subject of that kind of unnerving scrutiny before and, in spite of herself, she stiffened. No one in Montluce would dare to look at her like that.

'Forgive me for saying so, but you don't look desperate,' said Corran McKenna. He nodded at the high tech walking trousers and microfleece she'd bought in Glasgow only four days earlier. 'Those clothes you're wearing are brand new, and the labels tell me they weren't cheap. Besides,' he said, 'you're not suitable for the job.'

'Why not?'

'You're not a man, for a start.'

'That's not a good enough reason,' said Lotty, who might not want to rely on her royal status to protect her, but didn't have to like his dismissive tone. 'I think you'll find there's such a thing as sex discrimination.'

'And I think you'll find I don't give a toss,' said Corran. 'I need someone strong enough to do physical work, not someone whose most strenu-ous activity is probably unscrewing her mascara.'

Lotty's eyes sparked with temper. All at once she could feel her celebrated ancestors ranging at her back.

'I'm not wearing mascara,' she said coldly, 'and I'm stronger than I look.'

For answer, Corran McKenna reached out and took her hands, turning them over as if they were parcels so that he could inspect them. His fingers were long and blunt, and they looked huge hold-ing her small hands. He ran his thumbs over her palms and Lotty burned at the casualness of his touch.

'Please don't try and tell me that you've ever done a day's rough work in your life,' he said.

'That doesn't mean I can't start now.' Lotty tugged her hands free. 'Please,' she said, trying to ignore the way her palms were still tingling. If she looked down, she was sure she would be able to see the impression of his fingertips seared onto her skin. 'I really need this job.'

'*I* really need someone suitable,' said Corran. 'I'm sorry, but the answer is still no. And don't bother looking at me like that with those big eyes,' he added crisply. 'I'm immune.'

Her jaw actually dropped. 'I'm not looking at you like… like anything!'

She did astounded very well, but Corran found it hard to believe that she could really be unaware of the power of those luminous grey eyes. They were extraordinarily beautiful, the colour of soft summer mist, and fringed with long black lashes that did indeed appear to be natural when he looked closely.

The kind of eyes that got a man into trouble. Big trouble.

She was very pretty, slender and fine-boned, and she wore her trekking gear with an elegance that sat oddly with the short, garish red hair. A soft scarf at her throat added a subtle sophistication to her look.

Corran had the best of reasons for distrusting sophistication.

Frowning, he looked behind her for a car, but the overgrown gravel drive was empty. 'How did you get here?'

'I walked from the hotel,' she said, eyeing him warily.

'It didn't occur to you to ring beforehand?' he asked, exasperated. 'It would have saved you a pointless walk.'

'My phone doesn't work here,' she said.

'If it's a mobile, it won't. That's why we still have landlines,' he explained as if to a child.

'Oh.'

She sounded disconcerted. Corran could almost swear she had never used an ordinary telephone in her life. Maybe she hadn't. Privilege was written in every line of her face, in the tilt of her chin, and cheekbones like that only came from generations of aristocratic inbreeding.

He hardened his heart against the pleading in those huge grey eyes. Desperate? She was probably down to her last hundred thousand.

'Oh, well…I like to walk,' she said, recovering.

'You look ready to drop,' Corran told her frankly. 'How far have you walked today?'

'Sixteen miles.'

Great. Sixteen miles, and he was supposed to let her walk back to the hotel? Corran sighed in exasperation as he faced up to the inevitable. 'What's your name?'

'Lotty,' she said. A moment of hesitation. 'Lotty Mount.'

Now why didn't he believe her? 'All right, *Lotty,* you wait there. I'll get my keys.'

Her face lit up. 'You're going to let me stay?'

'No,' said Corran, ignoring the disturbing kick of his pulse. 'I'm going to drive you back to the Mhoraigh Hotel.'

She looked at him in dismay as she waved at the midges. 'I don't want to go back there!'

'Frankly, I don't care what *you* want,' he said, irritated that he had actually started to feel guilty there for a moment, irritated even more by the fact that his pulse still hadn't quite settled. '*I* want you off my property. There's no way you can walk back to the hotel and my reputation's bad enough round here without you collapsing halfway.'

'I'm not going to collapse,' she protested. 'And I've no intention of getting in a car with you,' she added as an afterthought.

'It's a bit late to start having scruples, having walked all the way out here,' Corran pointed out. 'There's just me and the dogs.'

'Well, anyway, I'd rather walk back,' Lotty said stiffly. 'It's a nice evening.'

Corran glanced up at the sky. As so often in Scotland, the day had started murky, but cleared in the afternoon, and now, at almost seven, only a few wispy clouds lurked low on the horizon. At this time of year it wouldn't get dark for hours yet. The hills were a soft blue, the water still and silver, the air almost golden. Lotty was right. It was a fine evening.

But there was not a breath of air to riffle the surface of the loch, which meant no breeze to blow the curse of the Highlands away.

'The midges will eat you alive,' he said, watching her slap at her neck below her ear. 'If they haven't already.'

'I'll be fine.' She lifted her chin. 'I'd rather walk,' she added and bent to heave the rucksack onto her back. Corran saw her wince at the weight of it on her shoulders, and he scowled.

'Don't be ridiculous, woman,' he said irritably. 'You can't walk all the way back if you've already done sixteen miles today.' He pointed a finger at her. 'Stay there. I'm going to get my car keys.'

He was gone less than two minutes, but by the time he came back Lotty was already toiling up the track.

'Fine!' he shouted after her. '*Be* stubborn! Just don't collapse on my land!'

'I won't,' she called over her shoulder.

Frustrated, Corran stood at the door and watched the slight figure. Her head was held high, but he could tell what an effort it was, and he swore again.

What was she thinking, hiking three miles to a strange house just on the off chance of a job? It wasn't safe. He could be anybody.

Corran glowered. He had enough problems of his own without worrying about Lotty, if that really was her name, but he watched her with a frown in his eyes until she had rounded the bend. He would give her half an hour or so and then go and see how far she had got. She would have proved her point by then, and would no doubt be more than grateful for a lift.

But when he drove along the track later, there was no sign of her. He went all the way to Mhoraigh, although he didn't go inside the hotel. The locals had made it quite clear what they thought of him, and if she had made it that far, she was perfectly safe.

The girl wasn't his responsibility, anyway. Putting the Land Rover into a three point turn, Corran headed back to Loch Mhoraigh House and told himself he wasn't going to think any more about her.

Still, he slept badly, and he was in an irritable mood when he set off for the cottages the next morning. The dogs ran eagerly ahead, past the old stable block and the walled garden, past the ruined boathouse and the track leading up to the barns and out beside the loch to the dilapidated cottages that had been built by his great-great-grandfather for the estate workers in the days when Loch Mhoraigh had been a thriving estate.

It had rained during the night, and the air was fresh and sweet with the smell of bracken from the hills. Corran thought longingly of the high corries, but he couldn't afford to take a day off, especially now that he would have to advertise for more help. Gary had only lasted two days. That made him think about the girl, Lotty, and he shook his head. Quite how she had expected to do the job, he didn't know. She didn't look strong enough to lift that rucksack.

Although she had, now he came to think of it.

He would finish the plastering in the first cottage, Corran decided, then he would advertise in the local paper—again. He could do that online. He was mentally composing an advert that made the job sound attractive while simultaneously making it clear that the successful applicant would have to work till he dropped for a meagre wage when he realised that Meg had frozen at the cottage door, which stood open although Corran knew that he had closed it when he left the day before.

Meg dropped to her belly and lay alert and quivering as Corran came up. He frowned. 'What is it, Meg?' He looked around him, and his brows drew even closer together. 'And where's that other damned dog?'

Telling Meg to stay, he stepped inside the cottage. The door on the left led into the living room, and there, sure enough, was his mother's dog, fawning over the girl who had turned up on his doorstep the night before.

The girl whose stricken expression had sent him on a fool's errand to the village just to make sure that she hadn't collapsed in a heap in the middle of the track.

For a long moment, Corran couldn't trust himself to speak.

She had abandoned her rucksack somewhere, and was in the same clothes she had worn the day before, except that now the scarf was knotted around her head like a Fifties housewife, which should have looked absurd but somehow looked chic instead. Her sleeves were rolled up in a businesslike way. She had clearly been sweeping up sawdust, and she still held the broom in her hands as she crouched down to make a fuss of the dog.

At Corran's entrance, though, she straightened. 'Good m-morning,' she said brightly, and he heard the slight stammer he'd noticed yesterday. Corran guessed that it only happened when she was nervous.

As well she might be.

'What the hell are you doing here?' he demanded, which he thought was fairly restrained under the circumstances.

'Well, I could see you've been working in here, so I thought I could start c-clearing up.'

'Oh, did you? And what part of me telling you that I wasn't going to give you a job and wanted you off my property didn't you understand?'

The soft mouth set in a stubborn line. 'I wanted to prove that I could do the job. All I'm asking is a chance to show you what I can do.'

'I drove all the way to Mhoraigh last night in case you'd collapsed on the track,' Corran told her furiously. 'Are you telling me you were here all the time?'

'There was some straw in the barn. I slept there.'

It had easily been the most uncomfortable night of Lotty's life. In spite of her exhaustion, she hadn't slept at all. Late in May, the night had still been cool and, even wearing all her clothes, she had been cold and bitterly regretting that she had ever heard of Loch Mhoraigh.

Why hadn't she tried harder to persuade the hotel to give her a job of some kind, just until she had earned enough to move on to Fort William? But she had chosen to come out here, and now pride wouldn't let her accept Corran McKenna's casual dismissal. She might not be using her title, but she was still a princess of Montluce.

Not that pride had been much comfort as Lotty had shivered on the straw and suffered the midges that swarmed through the cracks in the old barn doors. Now she wanted nothing so much as a shower and a cup of coffee.

But first she had to convince Corran to let her stay.

He wasn't looking at all encouraging. His brows were drawn together in a ferocious glare and his mouth set in what could only be called an un-compromising line. Lotty couldn't, in truth, really blame him for being angry, but how was she to know that he would be chivalrous enough to drive out and make sure that she was all right? If he was going to be nice, why couldn't he just give her the job?

It was time to be conciliatory, she decided. Some victories were won by battles, but sometimes ne-gotiation won just as effective a result. Lotty had learnt that from her family history too.

'Look, I'm sorry,' she said. 'I know I'm trespass-ing, but I can do this job—I *can!*' she insisted at Corran's expression. 'Gary—the guy I met at the hotel—told me he'd been cleaning and painting, and I can do that.

'You don't even need to pay me,' she went on quickly as Corran opened his mouth. 'I heard you can't afford to pay much in the way of wages, and

I'm prepared to work in exchange for somewhere to stay.'

He paused at that, and she pressed on, encouraged. 'Why not give me a chance? I'm not going to cost you anything, and I'm better than no one, surely?'

'That rather depends on how useful you can be,' he said grimly. 'I hope you're not going to try and tell me you've got any building experience?'

'I know how important it is to keep a building site clean,' said Lotty, who had once laid the foundation stone of a new hospital and had been impressed by the neatness of the site. She'd assumed that it had been tidied up for her arrival, as things usually were, but the foreman had assured her that wasn't the case. He wouldn't tolerate mess on his site at any time. 'An untidy site is a dangerous site,' she quoted him to Corran.

'And just how many building sites have you been on?' he asked, clearly unconvinced.

Lotty thought of the construction sites she'd been shown around over the years. Her father, the Crown Prince, had been more interested in Ancient Greece than in modern day Montluce, and after her mother had died it had fallen to Lotty to take on the duties of royal consort.

'You'd be surprised,' she said.

Corran studied her through narrowed eyes. 'Would I, indeed?'

Oh, dear, she was supposed to be allaying his suspicions, not arousing them. Lotty bent to pat the little dog who was fussing at her ankles still.

'Look, I can see that in an ideal world you'd employ someone with building skills,' she said, 'but I gather experienced tradesmen aren't exactly queuing up to work for you, so why not give me a try until you find someone else? What can be so hard about cleaning and painting, after all? And at least my services will come free.'

Corran was thinking about what she'd said, Lotty could tell. She held her breath as he rubbed a hand over his jaw until she began to feel quite dizzy. It might have been lack of oxygen but it was something to do with that big hand too, with the hard line of his jaw. It didn't look as if he had shaved that morning and Lotty found herself wondering what it would be like to run her own hand down his cheek and feel the prickle of stubble beneath her fingers.

The thought made her flush and she tore her gaze away and got her breathing back in order. Taking a firmer hold of the broom, she went back to tidying up the curls of wood and sawdust that covered the floor. No harm in giving Corran McKenna a demonstration of what she could do. It might not be the most skilled job in the world, but a quick look round the cottage had shown her that there was plenty of cleaning to be done.

'I'm not denying that I've found it hard to find anyone prepared to stick the job longer than a few days,' Corran said at last.

'I gather you might need to work on your management skills,' said Lotty, still sweeping.

'I see you and Gary had a good chat!' Corran snorted in disgust. 'All he had to do was plaster a few walls. Why the hell would he need *managing?*'

'Well, you know, an encouraging word every now and then might have helped,' she suggested before she could help herself. 'Not that I'd need any encouragement,' she added hastily.

'No encouragement, no money...' Corran watched her brushing ineffectually at the floor and looked as if he couldn't understand whether to be intrigued or exasperated. 'I don't understand why you're so keen to work here. Why not look for a job where you'd get paid at least?'

'I can't afford to go anywhere else.' She might as well tell him, Lotty decided. 'I lost my purse yesterday.'

It had been so stupid of her. She just wasn't used to being careful about her things. There was always someone who would pick things up for her, deal with settling any bills, check that she hadn't left anything behind.

'I haven't got money for a cup of coffee, let alone a bus fare.'

Corran's look of suspicion only deepened. 'When most women lose their purses they go to the police,' he pointed out. 'They don't set off into the wilds to doorstep strange men, insist on jobs they're not qualified to do, and trespass on private property!'

Lotty flushed. 'I'm sorry, but I didn't know what else to do.'

'What about calling your bank or credit card company for a start?'

How could she explain that a phone call to her bank would likely have led straight back to

Montluce, where her grandmother would have the entire security service looking for her?

'I don't want anyone to know where I am,' she said after a moment.

Corran's black brows snapped together. 'Are you in trouble with the police?' he asked.

For a moment Lotty toyed with the idea of pretending she had pulled off a diamond heist, but she abandoned it regretfully. Corran's eyes were too observant and she would never be able to carry it off.

'It's nothing like that.' She moistened her lips. She would have to tell him something. 'The thing is, I…I needed to get away for a while,' she began carefully.

It went against the grain to lie, and her grandmother would be horrified at the idea of her denying her royal heritage, but Lotty was determined to spend the next few weeks incognito.

'My mother always talked about the time she walked the Highland Way, and I thought it would be a good idea to walk it for her again, the way I always told her I would, and think about what I wanted to do with my life.'

So far, so true. Lotty had spent long hours sitting with her mother when she was dying. She had held her thin hand and kept a reassuring smile on her face all the time so that her mother wouldn't worry. She'd only been twelve, but she hadn't once cried the way she wanted to, because her grandmother had told her that she was a princess of Montluce and she had to be as brave as all the princesses before her.

There was no need to tell Corran about giving her close protection officer the slip in Paris, or about the crossing to Hull, where she was fairly sure she wouldn't meet anyone she knew, and where she'd had her hair cut in a funny little place upstairs on a side street.

She had dyed it herself that night, just to make sure she was unrecognizable, but the colour wasn't anything like it had promised on the box. She had been horrified when she looked in the mirror and saw that it had gone bright red. She looked awful! The only comfort was that no one would ever, ever associate Princess Charlotte with red hair. She was famous for her sleek dark bob and stylish wardrobe, and there was certainly nothing sleek or stylish about her now.

Apart from the hair fiasco, Lotty had been

pleased with herself that night. She had got herself across the Channel, and she was on her own. Not a huge adventure for most people, but for Lotty it was a step into the unknown. She was free!

Only sitting in that tiny hotel room, Lotty had realised that now there was no one to organize her day for her, she didn't quite know what to do with herself. That was when the idea of walking the Highland Way her mother had loved so much had jumped into her head. She had taken a train to Glasgow the next day, left her case in a locker at the station, and set off with a rucksack on her back.

'It was wonderful,' she told Corran. 'There's a very clear track, and other people are walking. I was having a great time, until I stopped for lunch yesterday. I had a sandwich at a pub, so I must have had my purse there, but when I got to the hotel at Mhoraigh I realised that I didn't have it any more. They were so kind at the hotel, and looked up the phone number of the pub for me, but, when I rang, they didn't know anything about my purse. I'd hoped someone might have found it and handed it in.'

She actually looked surprised that her purse,

clearly stuffed with cash and platinum credit cards, hadn't been handed back to her intact! She was the most extraordinary mix of sophistication and naivety, thought Corran.

He'd been listening to her story, unsure what to make of her. Clearly, she wasn't telling him everything with all this vague talk of *getting away*. It occurred to him that she might be a celebrity who needed to hide away from the media for a while. Not because he recognised her—Corran had no interest in the so called high life, as his ex wife could attest—but because there was a starry quality to her somehow, a certain purity to her features and a luminous presence that even her dusty, straw-flecked fleece and the insect bites on her face couldn't disguise.

She reminded him of the roe deer he had seen from his bedroom window early that morning. It had paused in a pool of light and lifted its head, graceful and wary. Lotty had the same kind of innocence in her eyes, an innocence that didn't go with the expensive clothes and the style with which she wore that ridiculous scarf around her head.

Then he caught himself up. What was the matter

with him? Any minute now he'd be spouting poetry when what he *should* be doing was remembering just how easily a beautiful woman could tie you up in knots. Corran scowled at the memory. Nothing Lotty had told him had made him any less suspicious of her motives.

CHAPTER TWO

'Go on,' he said grimly. 'You're at the hotel, and have discovered that—incredibly—nobody has handed in your purse.'

'So I was stuck,' said Lotty. 'But then I met Gary, and he told me about this job, and it seemed *meant*. I needed a job, you needed someone to work for you. I walked all the way out here, but then you wouldn't even *consider* me, and I just couldn't face going back to the hotel, so I found somewhere to sleep and, if it's any comfort, I got bitten to death by midges.' She showed him her bare forearms, where she had been scratching.

Corran refused to be sympathetic. 'Serves you right,' he said callously. 'If you'd been sensible, you could have had a lift back to the hotel and called someone from there.'

'I'm not going to call anyone,' Lotty said, her face set. 'I can't explain, but I just *can't*.' She turned the full force of those lovely grey eyes on Corran, who had to physically brace himself against them. 'Oh, *please*,' she said. *'Please* let me stay. It would just be for a few weeks.'

'Weeks?'

'Until you can get someone else, at least,' she amended quickly.

Corran managed to drag his eyes from hers at last and sighed. 'Come with me,' he said, making up his mind abruptly.

Propping her broom against the wall, Lotty followed Corran out of the cottage where they were met by a black and white collie.

'This is Meg,' said Corran. '*She* does what she's told.'

Lotty thought that she was being obedient too but, after a glance at Corran's face, she decided not to point that out. He was as formidable as the bare hills that rose on either side of the loch. It was a shame he didn't smile more, especially with that mouth…

Hastily, she looked away.

It didn't matter whether Corran smiled or not as long as he let her stay. The alternative was to admit that she really was just a pampered princess who couldn't cope on her own. All she would have to show for her rebellion would be four days walking.

Compared to that, what did it matter if Corran smiled or not?

He led her to one of the other cottages strung out along the lochside. It was the same sturdy shape as the others, with low, bumpy stone walls, their white paint now flaking sadly, and dormer windows set in the roof like a pair of quirky eyebrows.

'Take a look,' said Corran, opening the front door and gesturing her through with an ironic flourish of his hand.

Lotty stepped cautiously inside. The cottage was filthy. It was cluttered with broken furniture and shrouded in ghostly grey cobwebs. In the kitchen, the sink was stained and rusty, there was mould growing under the old fridge, and the floor was covered with mouse and bird droppings. A window hung open, its glass cracked and dirty, and the banister was smashed. Afraid to trust the creaking floorboards, Lotty turned slowly in one spot.

'What do you think?' asked Corran.

'It…needs some work.'

'Of all five cottages, this is the one in the best condition.' A grim smile touched the corners of his mouth at Lotty's expression. 'At least it doesn't need major work, and the roof is sound enough. I've got three months to get them all ready to let before September.'

'Three months? It would take three months to get rid of the dirt in this one room!' said Lotty.

'It's a pity you think that, because I was going to offer you a deal,' said Corran.

'A deal?'

'You get this cottage cleaned up and ready for painting by the end of the week, and I'll let you stay. I don't for a minute think you'll last that long, but, if you do, then you can paint it too, and then you can move on to the other cottages.' He looked at Lotty. 'Think you can do that?'

Lotty pursed her lips and pretended to study the room as if she were calculating how long it would take her, although the truth was that she had no idea how she would even *begin* to clean up that mess. Corran had clearly set her what he thought was an impossible task.

Raoul the Wolf wouldn't back down from a challenge like this, and neither would she.

'And in return?' she said with a fair assumption of casualness.

'In return you get board and lodging. You said you'd work for free, so that's the deal. Take it or leave it. Frankly, short of carrying you bodily back to the hotel, I can't think of another way to get rid of you!'

Nobody had *ever* spoken to Lotty the way Corran did. And no one was ever that unreasonable either. There was no way she could get this cottage ready for painting in three days. That was why he had set it as a challenge, one he knew she would fail.

She was just going to have to show him how wrong he was.

'I'll take the deal,' she said.

'You'll regret it,' Corran warned.

Lotty lifted her chin and met his pale eyes. 'Well, we'll see, won't we?'

'We will,' he agreed. 'I'm betting you won't make it to the end of the day, let alone the end of the week.'

'And I'll take that bet as well,' said Lotty defiantly.

Perhaps it wasn't fair. The man wasn't to know

that he was betting against a descendant of Léopold Longsword, after all. Fairness had been dinned into Lotty almost as thoroughly as pride and duty but, right then, she didn't care. 'I say I'll still be here at the end of the *month!*'

Corran's mouth twisted in a sardonic smile. 'You're really prepared to bet on that?'

'I am.' The grey eyes were bright with challenge. 'How much?'

'Well, as we know you don't have any money, that's not much of an issue, is it? What have you got to wager?'

Lotty thought of her wealth, safely squirrelled away, of her expensive car and designer wardrobe, of the antiques and valuable paintings that filled her palace apartment, of the priceless jewellery she had inherited as Princess of Montluce.

'My pride,' she said. He wasn't to know just how important self-respect was to her right then.

Corran held her gaze for a moment. 'Fair enough,' he said. 'If you're prepared to risk it, that's up to you.'

'And what will I get when I win?' she asked him.

'It's academic, but what would you like?'

Lotty searched her mind desperately. 'When I've been here a month you have to…to…to take me out to dinner,' she improvised.

Corran didn't exactly smile, but there was a glimmer of amusement in the pale blue eyes. 'It looks like we've got ourselves a deal, then,' he said. 'And you've got yourself a job—for as long as you can stand it.'

You'd have thought he'd offered her a diamond necklace instead of three days of unrelenting, dirty work for no pay.

'Oh, that's *wonderful!*' she said, her face lighting with a smile. '*Thank* you!'

Corran's chest tightened foolishly as he looked into her eyes, and for one ridiculous moment he forgot how to breathe properly. It was only a second before he got his lungs firmly back under control but, even so, it was an alarming feeling. She had only smiled, for God's sake!

Yanking his gaze from hers, he took out his confusion on the dog, who was worrying at a hole in the skirting board. 'Pookie! Get out of there!' he snarled, and the dog frisked over to him, its silky coat filthy now with dust and cobwebs.

Lotty looked at Corran. 'Pookie?'

He set his teeth. 'He's my mother's dog.' He eyed Pookie's not-so-white fluffiness with disgust. 'If you can call that a dog.'

Lotty had crouched down and was encouraging Pookie, who was now in a frenzy of excitement at all the attention, his little tail circling frantically as she ruffled his soft coat. 'He's sweet,' she said.

'He's not sweet,' snorted Corran. 'He's a nuisance. He's never been disciplined, and he's always filthy. I mean, who in their right mind has a *white* dog? I tried telling my mother this wasn't a suitable place for him, but she wouldn't listen. No, I have to put up with him for four months while she goes off on some world cruise! It's her fourth honeymoon, or possibly her fifth. I've lost count.'

'Well, he seems happy enough.' She studied the roughly shorn coat. 'I'm guessing he normally has a long coat?'

'And a ribbon to hold the hair out of his eyes,' said Corran sourly. 'I haven't got time to deal with any of that nonsense. I cut his coat as soon as my mother had gone. She'll have a fit when she comes back, but that's too bad. This is a working estate, and it's humiliating for Meg to be seen with a ball of fluff with a ribbon in its hair.'

Lotty laughed as she straightened. 'I can see Pookie doesn't do much for your image!' She looked around the filthy cottage. 'Well, I'd better get started if I'm going to get this ready for painting,' she said. 'Can I borrow the broom from the other cottage?'

'You might want to change your clothes first,' he said, frowning. 'It's going to be dirty work.'

'I don't have anything else with me. I just brought what I could carry in my rucksack.'

'I could probably find you an old shirt,' said Corran gruffly.

'Well...thank you,' said Lotty, with the smile that was famous throughout Montluce. 'If you're sure. I don't want to be any trouble.'

'It's a bit late for that,' he grumbled. 'You'd better come up to the house. I don't suppose you've had any breakfast either?'

'No,' she admitted and he blew out an exasperated breath.

'How were you expecting to work if you hadn't had anything to eat? You're no good to me if you're fainting with hunger.'

He stomped back to the house, Lotty following meekly in his wake, while Meg trotted beside him and Pookie scampered around in circles, yapping with excitement.

At the back door he kicked the mud and dust off his boots and snapped his fingers to the dogs. 'I'll feed these two, and maybe that will shut Pookie up. If you want to make yourself useful, you can make some tea. The kitchen's through there.'

He disappeared down a corridor hung with battered waxed jackets and mud-splattered boots, the dogs at his heels. There was something so incongruous about the big man with the fluffy little dog that Lotty couldn't help smiling as she watched them go. Corran might look tough, but he was also a man who couldn't say no to his mother. That made her feel better.

The kitchen was a square, solid room with fine proportions and a ceiling festooned with old-fashioned drying racks, but to Lotty it seemed bare and cheerless.

Not that she knew much about kitchens. All her meals were sent up from the palace kitchens, and if she wanted a cup of tea, she rang a bell and one of the maids made it in the servants' galley.

There was no bell to ring now, and no useful maid. Lotty looked around dubiously. She had never made tea or coffee before, but how difficult could it be?

Well, there was the kettle, at least. She carried it over to the sink, filled it and set it back on the base, resisting the urge to brush her hands together in self-satisfaction. Eat your heart out, Raoul the Wolf, she thought. He wasn't the only Montvivennes who could rise to a challenge.

Now, where was the tea? Aha! Lotty pounced on a pack, and was feeling pretty confident until she realised that the kettle wasn't getting hot. She put her hand on it, and had just bent her head to see if she could hear anything when Corran walked in and raised his brows at the sight of her with her ear pressed against the kettle.

'I don't think it's working,' she said as she straightened.

Corran looked at the kettle and then at her. Without a word, he reached round and clicked on a switch at the back of the kettle. Immediately, a light came on and there was a rushing noise.

Lotty bit her lip. 'I haven't used a kettle like this before.'

'Have you put a tea bag in a mug and poured over boiling water?' Corran asked sarcastically.

She hoped she didn't look too grateful for the tip. Bag, boiling water. She could do that. 'I don't suppose you've got any coffee?'

'There's instant.' He tossed her a jar, which she caught more by luck than science. 'Sorry, I'm fresh out of luxuries,' he said, correctly interpreting Lotty's look of dismay. She would have sold her soul for a cup of freshly ground coffee right then.

'I'll have tea,' he told her, opening a cupboard. 'The mugs are in here.'

'Have you just arrived?' Lotty took out two, leaving a single mug marooned in a vast cupboard. 'You don't have much stuff.'

'I moved in a couple of months ago.' Corran tossed a couple slices of bread in the toaster and slammed it down. 'I've never been a big one for *stuff*,' he told her. 'You don't acquire much in the Army, and my ex wife kept the house and all its contents when we got divorced.'

So he was divorced. Lotty filed that little bit of information away. She would have liked to have known more, but didn't want to sound too interested. It was hard to imagine Corran McKenna unbending enough to ask anyone to marry him.

Not her business, of course, but Lotty couldn't help wondering what his ex-wife was like as she put a tea bag in a mug and hoped she looked as if she knew what she was doing. What sort of woman would crack that grim façade? What would it take to bring a man like Corran McKenna to his knees? To make that hard mouth soften and the icy eyes warm with desire?

Lotty stole a glance at him as he opened the fridge and fished out butter and jam and a pint of milk, which he sniffed at suspiciously before putting it on the table. She wasn't at all surprised to hear that he had been in the Army. He had that tough competence she had seen in all her close protection officers, most of whom also came from a service background. They were all lean, hard men like Corran, men with absolute focus and eyes that were never still.

But she had never noticed their mouths before, or speculated about their love lives. Just looking at Corran's mouth made Lotty's stomach jittery. Why had she started to think about him kissing? Now warmth was pooling disturbingly inside her.

Lotty made herself look away and concentrated on unscrewing the jar of coffee granules instead.

'It's a shame this room is so bare,' she said to break the silence. Her voice sounded thin, as if all the air had been squeezed out of it. 'It could be a lovely kitchen.'

Corran grunted. 'The kitchen is the least of my worries at the moment. The rest of the house is just as bare. I'm more concerned about getting the estate up and running again. I can live without furniture until then.'

'You don't have any furniture?'

'Just the basics. This table. A couple of beds.' He nodded his head at the armchair by the range. 'That old chair my father's dog used to sleep on.'

'Then this was your father's house?'

'Yes,' said Corran, a curt edge to his voice. 'I inherited the house and the estate from him.'

'Isn't it usual to inherit the furniture as well as the house?'

He shrugged. 'My stepmother took everything when she moved to Edinburgh.'

'Why did she do that?'

'You'd have to ask her that,' he said distantly.

Lotty sniffed cautiously at the jar of coffee,

unable to suppress an involuntary moue of dis-
taste. She was trying to remember what the barmaid had told her at the Mhoraigh Hotel. 'I heard
there was some kind of family feud,' she told
Corran.

'It takes two to feud,' he said in a flat voice. *'I'm
not feuding.'*

Lotty had been spooning coffee granules into a
mug, but stopped when she saw Corran's expression. 'What?'

'You like your coffee strong.'

Uh-oh. Clearly she had overdone it. 'Er, yes…
yes, I do.' Surreptitiously, she spilled the last
spoonful back into the jar. 'They say the estate
should have gone to your brother,' she said to dis-
tract him.

'My half-brother,' he corrected her sharply.
'Who told you that? Oh, you'll have got it from
the hotel in Mhoraigh, of course,' he answered his
own question. 'That well-known centre of unbi-
ased information!'

'Is it true?'

'No, it's not true.' Corran scowled as he threw
a couple of plates on the table and rummaged in
a drawer for knives. Why should he care what

Lotty thought? She had pushed her way in here, and if she didn't like it, she could leave. It didn't matter if she believed that he wasn't entitled to the estate, but still he found himself saying, 'I'm my father's eldest son.' The words sounded as if they were pushed out of his mouth. 'I was born here.'

She had found a warm spot in front of the range and was leaning against it, her arms spread along the rail. 'You don't sound Scottish,' she commented.

'My parents divorced when I was six. My mother took me to London after that.'

'So Loch Mhoraigh isn't really home to you?'

'Yes, it is!' As always, the suggestion caught Corran on the raw. Mhoraigh was the only home he had ever had. 'I spent part of every summer here when I visited my father.'

Lotty was frowning. 'Then why is there a question mark over you having the estate? Doesn't the eldest son usually inherit?'

'It's normal, yes, but Andrew—my half-brother—is very popular around here. Especially at the hotel, where he seemed to spend most of his time as far as I can gather,' Corran added evenly.

'Everyone would much rather he had inherited the estate.'

'Why not you?'

He sighed. 'Are you always this nosy?'

For a moment she looked taken aback. 'I suppose I'm used to asking a lot of questions,' she said.

'As part of your job?'

Something uncertain flickered in her eyes. Good, thought Corran. Let her see what it was like being on the receiving end of an interrogation for a change!

'Yes,' she said after a tiny hesitation. She cleared her throat. 'I suppose you could say I'm in public relations.'

'Does that mean you'd be happy discussing your family with a stranger?'

That strange expression flitted across her face again. 'No, perhaps not. But we're not going to stay strangers, are we? We're going to be working together for a whole month so I can win that bet,' she reminded him. 'We might as well get to know something about each other. And I'd rather know the truth than rely on gossip.'

'The Mhoraigh estate is mine,' said Corran. 'That's all the truth you need.'

'I don't understand why they don't like you in the village.'

'Not everyone falls for my charm,' he snarled at her, and then wished he hadn't when she chuckled. She looked startlingly pretty when laughter warmed the patrician looks.

'Oh, I can see they might be able to resist your sunny disposition,' she said, 'but most people like things to be fair and, if you're the eldest son, it's fair that you inherited, surely?'

Corran blew out an exasperated sigh. He might as well tell her or she would never shut up about it.

'My father always intended to change the entail on the estate,' he said, making sure his voice was empty of all bitterness. He didn't want Lotty concluding that he was screwed up about all this, no matter how pretty she looked when she smiled.

'Andrew was his favourite. Everyone knew that. He had the huge advantage of not reminding him of my mother. My father never forgave her for leaving him, and every time he looked at me, he saw her. It made my visits…difficult.'

Lotty's lovely grey eyes darkened with sympathy. 'That must have been hard on you.'

'Please spare me the violins,' said Corran curtly. He couldn't bear people feeling sorry for him. He especially didn't want Lotty feeling sorry for him.

'I was perfectly happy as long as I could be here at Mhoraigh.' He had told himself that so often, he even believed it. 'I knew how my father felt and that the estate would go to Andrew eventually, and I'd accepted that. That's why I joined the Army. If I couldn't live here, I had no roots, and the military life suited me fine for a while. When my commission ended, though, I wanted to come back to the Highlands. I was thinking about buying a place of my own, and then my father sent for me.'

He stopped, remembering the last time he had seen his father. The churning bitterness and regret he had denied for so long. Why was he telling Lotty all this? What did it matter? He had come to terms with his father's rejection long ago.

Hadn't he?

'He told me that he wasn't going to change the entail after all. I still don't know why. Perhaps he thought the estate would be too much of a liability for Andrew. Mhoraigh would be mine, he said, but he was leaving everything else to my stepmother and Andrew. The trouble was that there was no money left after the way they'd all been living these past few years. I daresay Moira thought all the furniture was the least she deserved. Hence the empty house,' said Corran.

Lotty was a good listener, he realised. She kept her eyes fixed on his face and her head was tilted slightly to one side as she concentrated on what he was saying.

'It must have been a difficult situation for everyone,' she said.

'It wasn't difficult for me,' said Corran, rescuing the toast, which had started to burn. He flicked both slices onto a plate and offered them to Lotty, who pushed herself away from the range and came to sit at the table.

'I didn't care if they stayed or not, as long as I didn't have to actually live with them. I offered Moira Loch End House, which is a perfectly decent house, and said she could take any pieces of furniture she wanted, but she chose to go to Edinburgh instead, telling everyone that I'd thrown her out of her home.'

Lotty frowned. 'Why don't you tell everyone that's not the true story?'

'Because I don't care,' Corran said in a flat voice. He put more bread in the toaster and came back to sit at the table opposite Lotty. 'I understand why Moira is bitter. She always resented the fact that I existed when in her mind Andrew should have been the eldest. I was supposed to go away and not come back, but Mhoraigh was in my blood too.'

He didn't want to think about his annual visits to see his father, which he had longed for so much and hated at the same time. Andrew was seven years younger than him and the two boys had nothing in common. As a child, he had been bitterly aware that neither his father nor his stepmother wanted him there. Only the hills had welcomed him.

'As for the village, well, they've already made up their minds about me, and I haven't got the time or the inclination to try and make people like me. I've got enough to do keeping this estate afloat.'

Corran eyed Lotty with a mixture of resentment and frustration. He had been perfectly happy to keep all this buried until she had started asking her questions. What was it about her that made you want to *tell* her, to make her understand? It had to be something to do with that shining sincerity, that luminous sense of integrity that made you trust her in spite of the fact that you knew nothing about her.

'So what about you?' he asked, wanting to turn the tables once more. He pushed the butter and jam towards her. 'I suppose you come from a big, happy family where everybody loves each other and behaves nicely?'

Lotty understood the sneer in his voice. She understood the ripple of anger. She had heard a lot of sad stories in her time. No matter how people tried to dress them up for a royal audience, the pain was always there, and her heart ached for Corran as it did for everyone she met who had suffered and endured and who made her feel guilty for not having done the same.

She could only imagine what it had been like for Corran, loving this wild place but feeling unwanted here. No wonder there was still something dark and difficult in his face. For as long as she could remember, wherever Lotty went, people had tidied up and given her flowers and waved flags and clapped her just for existing. She might long for anonymity sometimes, but never had she been made to feel unwelcome.

She was lucky.

'I can't claim a big family,' she said, buttering her toast. The extended family wasn't even that big now, she thought, and it wasn't that happy either. She wondered what Corran would make of the so-called curse of the Montvivennes, which had seen such tragedy over the past couple of years.

'I'm an only child. I'd have loved to have had a brother or sister,' she added wistfully. It would have been wonderful to have shared the responsibility, to have had someone else who understood what it was like. 'My mother died when I was twelve, and my father last year.'

There was a pause. 'I'm sorry,' said Corran gruffly. 'I shouldn't have said that about happy families.'

'It's OK. Both my parents loved me, and they loved each other. That makes us a happy family, I think.'

'So you're on your own too,' he said after a moment.

Lotty had never thought of it like that before. As a princess, she was rarely alone.

'Well, there's my grandmother,' she said. 'And my cousin.' Philippe was like a brother, she thought.

And of course there were thousands of people in Montluce who loved her and thought of her as one of their own. She had no grounds for feeling alone.

'No husband? No boyfriend?'

'No.' Aware of Corran's eyes on her, Lotty felt the telltale colour creeping along her cheeks. She spread jam on her toast and took a bite. 'No, there's no one.'

'So who are you running away from?'

Still chewing, Lotty put down her toast. 'I'm not running away.'

'You said you needed to get away,' he reminded her.

She had. Lotty sighed. How could she explain to Corran the pressure to be perfect all the time?

Of course she wasn't running away from anything bad. Her life was one of unimaginable luxury and Lotty had always known that the price of that was to do her duty, and she did it.

Since her mother's death, her grandmother had controlled her life absolutely. Every minute of Lotty's day was organized for her, and Lotty went along with it all, because to protest would be childish and irresponsible.

How selfish would she be to insist on her own life when so many people looked forward to her visits? How could she behave like a spoilt brat when her own grandmother had devoted her entire life to the service of the country and endured bitter tragedy without complaint? The Dowager Blanche had lost two sons and a great-nephew in quick succession. Compared to that, how could Lotty say that she didn't want to open another hospital, or spend another evening shaking hands and being nice?

Until Philippe came back and the Dowager Blanche had decided that Lotty's duty to the country extended to marrying a man who didn't love her. Philippe had understood. It was Philippe who had encouraged her to escape. 'Your grandmother is the queen of emotional blackmail, Lotty,' he'd said. 'You deserve some fun for a change.'

'I've always been a good girl,' Lotty told Corran. 'I've always behaved well, and done what's expected of me. I just want a chance to be different for a while. I want to take the kind of risks I never take. I want to make my own mistakes. I want to see if I'm as brave as I think I am, and if I go home now I'll know I'm just a coward.

'I'm not running away,' she told him again. 'I just want to do something by myself. For myself.'

'Then you're going to learn what I learnt a long time ago,' said Corran. 'If you want something badly enough, the only person you can rely on is yourself.'

To Lotty, it sounded a cold philosophy, but how could she argue when she had no experience of relying on herself?

'And you want Mhoraigh?' she said.

Corran nodded. 'This used to be one of the finest estates in the Highlands,' he told her. 'But there's been no maintenance for years, and gradually its wealth has been frittered away. My father liked to act the laird, and he was big on shooting parties and keeping up traditions, but he didn't believe in getting his hands dirty, and Andrew's the same. He looks the part, but the land was just a source of income for him.

'But Mhoraigh's mine now,' said Corran, setting his jaw, 'and I'm going to make it what it was.'

'On your own?'

'On my own,' he agreed. 'Of course, it would be easier if I had some financial reserves, but between alimony payments and all the ready assets going to Moira and Andrew, I can't begin to improve the breeding stock or even keep up with the maintenance.

'That's why I need to get the cottages up and running as soon as I can,' he said, drumming the fingers of one hand on the table. 'Holiday lets are a good source of income, but the summer is my only real opportunity to get the work done. This is a working estate, and there's farming to be done too. We've finished lambing and the sheep are out on the hill now, but come September I need to be taking them to market. Then I'll be buying tups, and the cattle will go in October. And all that's apart from the forestry and routine maintenance.'

'Hmm,' said Lotty through a mouthful of toast. 'I can see why you need some help.'

'And instead I've got you,' Corran said with a sardonic look.

She met his eyes across the breakfast table. 'Yes,' she agreed. 'You've got me.'

CHAPTER THREE

AFTER breakfast, Corran showed Lotty to a room upstairs. He had warned her that the house was bare, but it was still a shock to see how thoroughly it had been stripped by his stepmother. There were no carpets or curtains, hardly any furniture, and tired patches on the walls marked where pictures had once hung.

It made Lotty feel sad to think of how bitter his stepmother must have felt to have left the house in such a state. Corran put on a good show of not caring what anyone thought, but Lotty had seen the bitter curl of his mouth when he had talked about being the unwanted son. Small wonder that he had grown into a grimly self-sufficient man.

Like the rest of the house, her bedroom was sparsely furnished, with just a bed and a straight-backed chair on the bare boards, but it was light and spacious and from the window there was a lovely view of the loch. Lotty, who had spent her life in the most luxurious of accommodation, was delighted with it.

She would have to collect her rucksack from the barn later, but for now Corran had provided her with an old shirt. Lotty took off her fleece and T-shirt and shrugged the shirt on over her bra, uncomfortably conscious of the feel of it against her bare skin. The cotton was worn and threadbare at the cuffs and collar, but it was clean and it smelt very comforting. She rolled up the sleeves and tried not to think that the skin the shirt had touched had been Corran's. It felt disturbingly intimate to be wearing his clothes.

Back at the cottage, she squared her shoulders determinedly and set to work, glad of the gloves she had brought in case the weather turned unseasonably cold. She would show Corran McKenna what she could do, but that didn't mean she had to like touching all the filth and horrible cobwebs.

She spent the first two hours dragging the clutter of old furniture in the living room outside. One or two of the bigger pieces would have to wait until she could persuade Corran to help her, but in the meantime at least she could start to make an impression. She rolled up rugs, coughing and spluttering at the dust, and then gritted her teeth before tackling the cobwebs on the ceiling with a broom.

Some of the spiders were enormous, and she had to jump out of the way as they scuttled irritably across the floor. Lotty hated spiders, but she wouldn't let herself scream. Princesses didn't squeal or shriek or make a fuss, and they were never afraid. Her grandmother had taught her that.

Once the spiders were dealt with, she even began to enjoy herself. She was grimy and hot and the dust made her wheeze, but there was no one to charm, no one waiting to shake her hand, no one expecting anything of her except that she get this job done. No deference, no sycophancy, just Pookie, who seemed to have attached himself to her and was snuffling happily around, scrabbling at holes in the skirting boards and growling at imaginary rats.

At least Lotty hoped they were imaginary.

When Corran found her at lunchtime, she was sweeping up piles of dust and rubbish and singing tunelessly in French while Pookie pounced on fluff balls. Neither of them noticed him at first, which just went to show what a useless excuse for a dog Pookie was.

From the doorway, Corran watched Lotty wielding the broom inexpertly. She was swamped by his shirt, and she wore that scarf twisted up and knotted in two corners, so she should have looked ridiculous. Instead, the rough shirt just emphasised the delicacy of her arms and the pure line of her throat rising out of the worn collar, while she managed to make even the scarf look chic.

And she was singing! She wasn't supposed to be happy. She was supposed to be overwhelmed by the task he had set her, and disgusted by the dirt. She was supposed to be giving up and going away. He needed help, yes, but he needed someone practical, not this slight, elegant figure with her spine of steel and her speaking grey eyes. Lotty was too…distracting.

Look at how she had made him talk over breakfast, pushing him to think about the past, and look at him now, breaking off to make coffee, just to make sure she stopped for a few minutes! He didn't have time to worry about her.

Corran scowled and rapped on the door with his knuckles. 'I've brought lunch,' he said curtly.

JESSICA HART
67

Startled, Lotty swung round in mid-song, and Pookie came scampering over to yap and fawn at his knees to cover his embarrassment at being caught unawares.

'Quiet!' Corran bellowed and the dog dropped back on its haunches, ears drooping comically in dismay at his tone.

'He's just pleased to see you,' said Lotty, smiling. She propped her broom against the broken banister, pulled off her gloves and dropped them on the bottom step, and came towards him, brushing her hands on her shirt. On *his* shirt. 'And I am too, if you've got lunch with you!'

When she smiled, her whole face lit up and Corran felt something tighten around his heart for a moment. It was a long time since anyone had looked happy to see him.

And how pathetic was it that he had even thought of that?

'Don't expect me to make a habit of it,' he said, glowering. 'It's just that I've finished plastering and I thought I might as well throw some sandwiches together. I want to start baling silage this afternoon, and there's no point in stopping for lunch once I get going.'

'I didn't think I'd be allowed the time for lunch,' she said. 'I certainly didn't think you'd make it. I'm impressed by the service!'

That was right, Corran thought, hunching a shoulder. Make a big deal of it, why didn't she? Next she would be suggesting that he was worried that he might have asked her to do too much.

'It's not too bad outside,' he said stiffly. 'I thought we could eat down by the loch.'

'That's a wonderful idea!' said Lotty. She took a deep breath of fresh air, glad to get out of the musty cottage for a while, although she had no intention of admitting that to Corran, of course. Putting her hands to the small of her back, she stretched, unable to prevent a tiny grimace at the twinge of her muscles.

'Had enough?' said Corran.

'Certainly not,' she said, determined not to let him guess how grateful she was for the chance to stop for a while. 'You were the one who stopped for lunch!'

Lotty's shoes crunched on the shingle as she made her way back up the little beach after washing her hands in the cool, clear loch. Corran was unwrapping a packet of sandwiches on the rocky outcrop.

'It's nothing fancy,' he warned as he held out the packet to her.

Lotty took one and perched on the rock beside him. 'It looks great to me,' she said honestly. She couldn't believe how hungry she was, after all that toast at breakfast too.

The sandwich was little more than a piece of cheese thrown between two pieces of ready-sliced bread, but Lotty had rarely enjoyed a lunch more. It felt good to be outside. The air was cool and faintly peaty and she pulled off her scarf so that the breeze could ruffle her hair.

Taking a mouthful of sandwich, she turned up her face to the sun that was struggling through the clouds. 'Good,' she mumbled. Even that small rebellion felt wonderful. Princesses *never* talked with their mouths full. When she went home she would have to remember her manners, but right now she could do whatever she wanted. It was an exhilarating thought.

Corran was pouring coffee from a flask into plastic mugs, but he put it down so that he could brush a cobweb from Lotty's shoulder. 'You're filthy,' he said.

It was a careless touch, but Lotty's skin tightened all the same and she was conscious of a zing of awareness.

'That's what happens when you try and get rid of forty years' of dirt,' she said, embarrassed to find that she was suddenly breathless.

It wasn't as if Corran was particularly attractive. He was as hard and unyielding as the rock they were sitting on. The dark brows were drawn together over the pale, piercing eyes in what seemed a permanent frown. And yet one graze of his fingers was enough to send the blood skittering around in her veins, one look at his mouth and her heart bumped alarmingly against her ribs.

Unaware of her reaction, Corran handed her a mug. 'I couldn't remember how you took your coffee this morning, so I put milk in.'

'It doesn't make much difference to me,' said Lotty, glad of the excuse to shift her position on the rock. She wrinkled her nose as she looked down in the mug. 'I don't want you to think I'm not grateful, but this isn't what I call coffee.'

'I might have known you'd turn out to be a princess,' said Corran, and Lotty jerked, spilling most of the mug over his shirt.

'What?'

'You're very particular about your coffee.' His eyes sharpened suddenly. He was clearly putting something together. 'You were singing in French just now... I didn't guess because your English is perfect, but you're French, aren't you?'

Perhaps it would have been easier to have pretended that she was French, but pride in her country was ingrained in Lotty. 'I'm from Montluce,' she corrected him, chin lifting.

'Isn't that part of France?'

Lotty bridled. People *always* thought that. 'No, it isn't! We speak French, but Montluce is an independent state with its own monarchy.'

'And a big chip on its shoulder?' Corran suggested with a sideways glance.

'Not at all. We're small, but we have a very high opinion of ourselves!'

The corner of his mouth lifted. 'I see. Does everyone in Montluce speak such good English, or is it just you? I wouldn't have guessed if I hadn't heard you singing.'

'I was sent away to school in England after my

mother died,' she told him. 'You soon pick up the language when you have to.'

'Must have been tough to lose your mother and be sent to a strange country at the same time,' said Corran.

'It wasn't the best time of my life,' Lotty allowed, 'but I just had to get on with it.'

She had begged her father to let her stay with him in Montluce, but it was her grandmother who had dealt with all the practicalities of life after her mother's death. Lotty needed to speak English, the Dowager Blanche had decreed, and it would do her good to have a change of scene. The child was much too nervous as it was. She couldn't be allowed to mope around Montluce. Yes, her mother's death was sad, but Lotty had to learn to deal with whatever life handed her. There were to be no tears, no complaints. She was a princess.

So Lotty had gone away to school and she hadn't cried and she hadn't complained. But she had hated it.

'It was awful at first,' she said, sipping at her coffee in spite of everything she'd had to say about it. 'I don't know what I'd have done if I hadn't met my friend Caro there. We were both really plain and both horribly shy and, as if that wasn't bad enough, I had a stammer. I still stammer a little when I'm nervous,' she confessed.

'I noticed.'

Everyone else pretended that they didn't.

Corran's eyes rested on her face. 'You changed,' he said.

'I lost my puppy fat eventually and grew up,' she acknowledged.

'You did more than that. You're a beautiful woman,' said Corran in a matter-of-fact voice, 'as I'm sure you must know.'

Lotty heard that a lot. The beautiful Princess Charlotte. It made her uncomfortable. All beauty ever did was put her on a pedestal, where people gawped at her and admired her, but nobody got close enough to touch.

'I'd rather be pretty,' she said.

'Isn't beautiful better than pretty?'

'Pretty is warmer, less intimidating.' She stirred the shingle with the toe of her shoe. 'Being beautiful isn't the same as being desirable.'

'No,' said Corran thoughtfully after a moment. 'I suppose that's true.'

Not *but you're desirable, Lotty.* Not *I think*

you're wrong. I find beautiful women very desirable.

Well, what had she expected? Lotty chewed glumly on the second half of her sandwich. It was stupid to feel disappointed because he didn't think that she was desirable.

A pedestal could be a cold and lonely place. Thousands of people said they thought she was beautiful. Thousands loved her. But would they still love her, still want her, if they really knew her? Lotty wondered. If they could get past the mystique of royalty, past the security guards, past the rigid protocol of palace?

Lotty longed for someone to want her enough to try.

She longed to be desired, not for her title or her wealth, but for her body. She longed to know what it was like to love a man, to know what every other woman, it seemed, knew. What was the point of being beautiful if you could get to twenty-eight having barely been kissed? Lotty had never met a man who wasn't intimidated by the suffocating etiquette that surrounded her in Montluce. Sometimes it felt as if she was the only twenty-eight-year-old virgin in the world.

Dispiritedly, Lotty finished her sandwich and brushed the crumbs from her hands. Beside her, Corran was drinking his coffee, his eyes narrowed at the hills across the loch. The fingers around the mug looked very strong. He had a farmer's hands, square and capable and scarred with nicks and scratches. There was a focused quality to him, a forcefulness that sharpened the air around him and made it impossible to ignore even the smallest detail: the flat hairs at his wrist, the plaster dust in his hair, the creases edging his eyes.

He sat easily on the rock, long legs thrust ahead of him into the shingle, dusty boots crossed at the ankle. Never in a million years would Lotty have that assurance, that sense of being utterly at home in one's skin. Corran McKenna wasn't a man who would be intimidated by anything. If he wanted something, he would go out and get it.

He wouldn't care about mystique. If Corran wanted her, he wouldn't think twice about brushing aside her close protection team and knocking down her pedestal.

If Corran wanted to lose his virginity, he wouldn't bleat about how difficult it was to meet the right person. He wouldn't feel overwhelmed by ignorance or insecurity. He would reach out with those big hands and take what he wanted.

Lotty's mouth went dry and she swallowed, yanking her eyes away from that ruggedly un-compromising profile. It had taken all her courage to jump off her safe, lonely pedestal for a while. She might be descended from the likes of Raoul the Wolf and Léopold Longsword, but she wasn't brave enough to take the next step just yet.

She tipped the last of her coffee onto the shingle. 'I think I'd better get back to work,' she said in a hollow voice.

Afterwards, Lotty was never sure how she got through that first week at Loch Mhoraigh House. She had been tired before, but never with that bone-deep physical weariness that left her feeling leaden and light-headed at the same time.

Determined to prove Corran wrong that first day, she shut the doors and windows of the cot-tage once the midges gathered at four o'clock and began stripping off the peeling and faded wall-paper until her arms ached and her eyes bulged with exhaustion. Her grandmother had brought her up to do whatever needed to be done without complaint, and Lotty was going to stay there until she was finished.

'What are you still doing here?' Corran stomped into the cottage, slapping irritably at the midges. He had finished baling half an hour ago, and had expected to find Lotty back at the house. Having to come and find her had done nothing to improve his temper.

Slamming the door behind him, he took in Lotty, who was halfway up a stepladder, swaying alarmingly as she scraped at the sitting room wall. There were curls of wallpaper clinging to her scarf, and what little he could see of her face through the layer of grime was smudged with exhaustion. 'For God's sake, woman, get off that ladder before you fall off!'

'You told me I had to get the cottage ready for painting.'

'I didn't tell you to spend all night in here!'

'I will if that's what it takes.' Lotty jutted her chin at him in a stubborn gesture he was already finding familiar. 'There's no point in wasting the light when the evenings are long like this.'

'Don't be ridiculous,' Corran snapped. 'You're dead on your feet.'

'I'm all right,' she said, which was so patently untrue that he didn't even bother to argue.

'What about the dog?' He glared down at Pookie, who was scrabbling at his knees in the usual fawning welcome. Like Lotty, the dog was filthy, his white coat grey with dust and tangled with scraps of wallpaper and other rubbish. 'I don't suppose it occurred to you that he might need to be fed?'

As he'd intended, Lotty was instantly guilty. 'No, I didn't think of it. Sorry, Pookie.' She looked back at Corran. 'I don't suppose you could take him back with you and feed him now, while I finish this?'

'You suppose right,' he said. 'I want you to stop being so stubborn and come back to the house before you collapse.'

It was amazing how a mouth that looked so soft could set in such an implacable line. 'I want to finish this job.'

Corran had had enough. 'If you don't do as I say, I'm going to sack you, and then you won't *have* a job.' He jabbed his finger at her. 'Now, you get off that ladder *right now* or I'll come and drag you down myself!'

There was no mistaking that tone of voice. Lotty scrambled down from the ladder without another word. Nobody had *ever* spoken to her like that before and, even through her exhaustion, she was conscious of a flicker of shameful excitement. It was almost worth provoking Corran's temper to have the satisfaction of being treated so unlike a princess!

And the truth was that she wasn't sorry to be forced to stop. After a sixteen-mile walk the previous day, a sleepless night and the day's hard physical work, she was so tired she couldn't even muster the energy to brush the midges away, and she stumbled over her own feet until Corran took her arm in a hard grip.

'You are one stubborn woman, you know that?' he growled. 'Why don't you just admit that it's all too much for you?'

'Because it's not. I'm fine, honestly.'

'You can't even walk straight! This is exactly what I didn't want to happen,' he said grouchily. 'I haven't got time to worry about what sort of state you're in, you know. I can't concentrate on what I'm doing if I have to wonder about whether you've collapsed in a heap somewhere because you've got *no idea* how to be sensible!'

He harangued Lotty all the way back to the house, although she was too tired to take in much of it. As soon as they were inside and could shut the midges out, he let go of her arm and she slumped against the wall without his support. It was all she could do not to slide onto the floor with Pookie, who was yapping hysterically at the prospect of being fed.

Corran looked from one to the other as if unable to decide which of them was more exasperating. 'You!' He pointed at the dog. 'Shut up! And *you,*' he added to Lotty, jerking his finger at the ceiling, 'go up and have a bath. You've got half an hour before supper. And don't fall asleep in there!' he shouted after her as she bumped against the wall on her way to the stairs, the prospect of getting clean too delicious to resist.

The bathroom was draughty and as cheerless as the rest of the house, with linen fold panelling halfway up the walls and lino that curled at the corners. The cast iron tub had claw legs and rusty stains beneath the taps, but to Lotty it beat any five star bathroom hands down. She sank into the hot water with a groan of pleasure.

It felt as if every millimetre of her was caked with grime. Holding her breath, she squeezed her eyes shut and sank below the surface, to emerge smiling and spluttering a few moments later. It had been a long, tough day, but she had survived it. She had a job, she had somewhere to stay, and now she was going to be clean as well.

It felt wonderful.

Closing her eyes, Lotty rested her head against the rim of the bath and let her mind drift. And somehow it drifted to Corran, and the way he had looked when he had stormed into the cottage. He had obviously showered himself, because his dark hair had been damp still. His jeans emphasised his long legs and narrow hips, while the plain dark T-shirt moulded his broad chest.

Lotty had to admit that she liked his body. It was strong and solid, without being showy. She liked the easy way he moved, the feeling she had that he was utterly at home in his skin. She liked his competence, the assurance with which he did everything, even if it was just snapping his fingers at a dog or unscrewing a flask. Corran was in control of whatever he was doing.

He might not smile, but there was an appealing sureness to him. Lotty's mind floated further, back to the rock where she and Corran had shared lunch, back to wondering what he would be like as a lover.

If only she had more confidence! She was intelligent, capable, beautiful. She was a princess, for heaven's sake. By rights, she should have the nerve and the knowledge to seduce him without a second thought.

Not a single one of her distinguished ancestors would have hesitated to take what they wanted. But they hadn't had to be perfect, had they? They hadn't been brought up by Grandmère, hadn't been expected to take her mother's place and save her father distress by behaving perfectly at all times.

She didn't have to behave perfectly now, Lotty reminded herself.

The idea, terrifying in its recklessness, glimmered back into life. This was her chance, her one shot at living life like everyone else. For three short months, she could be normal.

And how normal was it to be a virgin at twenty-eight?

Maybe it was the hot water, but Lotty could feel herself beginning to glow. Perhaps she would never have the nerve, but she was allowed to dream, wasn't she?

She wanted to dream that she got out of this bath and went downstairs. In her dream, Corran was in the kitchen. Perhaps not the most romantic of settings, but it was the only room she had seen properly. Besides, there was something about all that tough masculinity in a domestic setting that appealed to her.

So, yes, he was in the kitchen, doing something ordinary. Cooking. Chopping something. Not onions or garlic, but something not quite so pungent. Tomatoes, perhaps. His head was bent and he was totally focused on his task, but when she appeared in the doorway, he lifted his head.

And he smiled.

Lotty had never seen Corran smile, not properly, but she knew it would be slow and sure, like the rest of him, and she shivered at the way it warmed the granite face, creasing his cheeks and curving that cool mouth.

Come here, he said, and in her fantasy his voice was dark and low and urgent. All the breath leaked out of Lotty's lungs just imagining it. It was a voice that would brook no disobedience, and it would never occur to her not to do exactly as he asked. So she would cross the kitchen towards him without taking her eyes off his and…

No, wait, what was she wearing? Lotty rewound a little. If she was going to have a fantasy, she might as well get it right, and she didn't want to lose her virginity in the jeans, camisole and raspberry-pink cashmere cardigan, which was all she had had to wear in the evenings for the last week. She certainly didn't want to be wearing her grungy work clothes.

Just a towel? She wouldn't have the nerve, Lotty decided. No, if this was a fantasy, she didn't have to be limited to the contents of her rucksack, did she? Her suitcase that was still sitting at Glasgow Station contained a Japanese print silk robe. She could wear that.

Satisfied, Lotty mentally slipped into the robe. Beneath it, she was naked and the silk felt cool against her bare skin. Ah, yes, now the fantasy was well back on track.

Come here, Corran said—again—and she walked towards him, the robe fluttering around her legs. She stood in front of him, and he reached wordlessly for the belt, tugging it gently so that the robe fell open.

Would he gasp at her beauty? Lotty considered and rejected this regretfully. She just couldn't imagine Corran gasping at anything. But he might smile again, mightn't he? A slow smile that started in his eyes and made her heart thump as he put his hard hands at her waist and drew her towards him.

And then—oh, then!—he would lower his head and—

'Lotty!' The door flew open and Corran charged into the bathroom.

Gasping with shock, Lotty jerked upright out of the water and slapped her hands to her shoulders to cover her breasts. 'What are you *doing?*' she shrieked.

'I thought you had drowned!'

He'd called her name. He'd knocked on the door. Silence. And then he'd remembered how tired she had been, because of him. He'd gone cold, picturing her sliding beneath the water, too tired to rouse herself, and he'd panicked, bursting into the room, convinced that he would find her limp and lifeless, desperately trying to remember resuscitation techniques.

And there she was, her eyes huge and frightened, her shoulders bare, and Corran's eyes had taken on a weird life of their own and were ensnared by the wet, glowing body in the bath, skidding from clavicle to earlobe to elbow to the arms clamped firmly over her breasts.

'I did knock,' he said, but his voice seemed to come from a long way away. He was disgusted with himself. He knew he had to get out of there, but he couldn't move. He didn't know whether he felt light-headed with relief or cold with anger.

Anger was easier to deal with. 'Why the hell didn't you answer?' he demanded.

'I didn't hear. I was d-daydreaming.'

The tiny stammer jolted Corran back to himself. *I still stammer a little when I'm nervous,* she had said.

She shouldn't be nervous of him, but what else could she feel when he had stormed into the bathroom and was standing there, staring at her?

Mortified, Corran forced himself to move at last. Turning his back on her, he strode for the door.

'Well, since you're alive after all, dinner's ready,' he said curtly.

'I—I'll be down in a minute.'

How long was it going to be before he got the image of Lotty in the bath out of his mind? That luminous skin, the wet, lovely slope of her shoulders. Her short hair was spiky, the grey eyes wide and startled, and a pulse had hammered in the bewitching hollow at the base of her throat.

Corran glowered as he drained the pasta. He'd been alone too long. The last thing he needed right now was a complication like Lotty.

She appeared a few minutes later, modestly covered in jeans and a cardigan. Not her fault that the soft pink wool seemed to hug her arms enticingly, reminding him of the bare skin beneath, or that the top she wore beneath the cardigan emphasised the delicate line of her clavicle.

Corran dragged his eyes away from it. 'I'm sorry about earlier,' he said stiffly.

'No, it was my fault,' she said. 'I didn't hear you and I might well have fallen asleep if you hadn't checked, so thank you.'

An awkward silence fell.

'It must have been some daydream,' he said to fill it. 'I was quite loud.'

A wash of colour swept up Lotty's throat.

Her eyes slid from his as she pulled out a chair and sat down. 'Something smells good,' she said, pointedly changing the subject, and Corran's interest was perversely piqued. What did a woman like Lotty dream about? he wondered.

Who did she dream about?

Well, it was none of his business, he reminded himself as he turned the pasta in the sauce. And he didn't care anyway. He had to remind himself of that too.

'Spaghetti bolognaise,' he told her, plonking the pot onto the table. 'I can only cook three dishes. This isn't going to be a great gastronomic experience for you.'

'I don't mind,' said Lotty, who was still jittery from the shock of Corran bursting into the bathroom. One moment she'd been dreaming *that,* and the next he'd been there, looking furious, and reality had slapped her around the face. This was no ardent lover. This was a man with far more on his mind than her pathetic little fantasies.

In one of those gruff acts of kindness that kept catching her unawares, he'd retrieved her rucksack from the barn and put it in her room. She felt a little better once she was dressed in the outfit she'd worn every evening on the walk, but she was still desperately aware of Corran moving around the kitchen and her breathing kept getting muddled up. His presence seemed to be sucking all the oxygen from the air. The only other person Lotty knew who had that same compelling presence was her tiny autocratic grandmother.

'Help yourself.' Corran gave her a plate and pushed the pot towards her. 'It'll be filling if nothing else.'

Lotty was still burning with embarrassment, but she took some pasta to be polite. The spoon and fork rang against the edge of the saucepan, loud in the silence.

A princess always puts people at their ease. The memory of her grandmother's voice was so clear that Lotty almost expected to turn and see her at her shoulder.

Clearing her throat, she forced herself to make conversation. 'Do you always cook for yourself?'

'I don't have much choice. Fortunately, I'm not

that bothered about food, but I get pretty sick of the same three dishes, I have to admit.' Corran paused in the middle of helping himself to pasta. 'I don't suppose you cook, do you?'

There was no use pretending. Lotty had barely been in a kitchen before arriving at Loch Mhoraigh. 'I'm afraid not.'

'Pity. I was going to suggest you might like to earn some extra money.'

'*Extra?*' Lotty raised her brows. 'I'm not earning *any* money, so how can I earn extra?'

'All right, maybe you'd like to earn *some* money on top of your board and lodging.' He looked at her assessingly. 'You could be my housekeeper. I can't pay much, mind, but it would be worth it not to have to do any more cooking myself for a while.'

'If you can afford to pay a housekeeper, why not give me something for cleaning the cottage?'

'That was a different deal,' said Corran. 'You wanted to do it. This is something I *don't* want to do. See the difference?'

Lotty chewed a mouthful of pasta. He was right. Filling was the best thing that could be said about it. Could she do much worse? The idea of earning her own money was ridiculously exciting for one who had been wealthy beyond most people's dreams since she was born.

Nearly as exciting, but not requiring nearly as much nerve as the idea of losing her virginity.

Over Corran's shoulder she could see a few tatty recipe books propped on the otherwise bare dresser.

'I can't claim any cooking experience, but I can read,' she said. 'I could have a go.'

'Great,' said Corran. 'Consider yourself hired.'

Lotty stared at him. 'Is that it?'

'I'm hardly going to give you an interview,' he pointed out. 'I don't care what the meals are like as long as they're edible and I don't have to cook them myself.'

It was a little late to start negotiating, Lotty realised, but she tried anyway. 'Do I get extra time to finish the cottage? It'll take me some time to do the cooking as well as the cleaning.'

Corran finished his mouthful as he considered. 'Fair enough,' he agreed at last. 'You can have an extra day. But that's all. Take it or leave it.'

Léopold Longsword would no doubt have wrung more concessions out of him in a process of wily

negotiations, while Raoul the Wolf would probably have just chopped his head off, but Lotty
took the deal.

CHAPTER FOUR

THERE were no curtains at her bedroom window. When the summer light woke her early in the mornings, Lotty would allow herself a few moments to just lie and remember where she was before she launched into another gruelling day. Her muscles ached, her bed was narrow, the mattress ancient and lumpy, the room bare, but she was very happy.

Every day was full of new experiences. Small ones, trivial ones, but for Lotty it was like discovering a new world. She learnt to peel potatoes and chop onions, to wash dishes and empty the vacuum cleaner. She wrote her first shopping list and got down on her knees with a scrubbing brush. Unable to bear the disgusting coffee, which Corran insisted was perfectly adequate, she even began to acquire a taste for tea instead.

It surprised her how quickly she fell into a routine. She would clear up after breakfast, prepare sandwiches for later and then head to clean the cottages. All morning she swept and brushed and scrubbed. The Dowager Blanche would be aghast if she knew that her granddaughter was on her knees like a servant.

There were times when Lotty had to screw up her nose. Times when she was so tired and filthy that she was tempted to take a break, but ironically those were the times when she remembered she was a princess. Proper princesses might not get dirty, but they didn't give up either.

So she kept going until she heard the tractor outside, which was her signal to join Corran for lunch. Once when it was raining, they ate their sandwiches in the barn, sitting on hay bales, but usually they went to the little beach and breathed in the tangy air that blew down the loch from the sea in the west.

Lotty was always stiff when she got up to head back for an afternoon's hard physical work in the cottages, but that was easy compared to the task of preparing a meal every evening. She was rather miffed to discover that she was not a natural cook. Montluce had a reputation for fine food that rivalled that of its more famous neighbour, France, and Lotty couldn't help feeling that she should somehow have acquired a talent for cooking along with the stubborn pride of all her countrymen.

The recipes never looked that difficult but, however closely she followed them, meat ended up charred or raw or horribly tough, while even a simple task like boiling vegetables resulted in either a challenging crunchiness or an unappetising slush. With every disaster, Lotty's chin inched a little higher, and the next day she would square up to the recipe book with renewed determination.

Luckily, Corran didn't seem that bothered. He had no interest in food and ate only to fuel himself as far as Lotty could see.

'Isn't there anything special you'd like me to make?' she asked him once.

'This is fine,' he said, forking in a beige sludge that was supposed to be pasta with a delicate cheese sauce.

'There must be something you like particularly,' she persisted.

Chewing, Corran gave it some thought. 'My father had a cook for a while—Mrs McPherson. She used to make the best scones.'

Scones. Well, that shouldn't be too difficult. Determined to make something Corran would enjoy, Lotty found a recipe. It looked fairly straightforward, but she would need bicarbonate of soda and cream of tartar, whatever *they* were.

She added them to the shopping list. Corran had a meeting with his father's solicitor in Fort William, and had told her to make a note of any essentials they needed so that he could get them in one big supermarket shop. At the top, Lotty had written: *'Decent Coffee!!!!'* Not that she expected Corran to take any notice.

It was just as well she had given up on the seduction idea, Lotty reflected every night as she fell into bed. She was too tired to put it into action.

If she worked hard, Corran worked even harder. He was always up before her, and was off checking his cattle before breakfast. The sheep grazed high up on the hills, but the cattle were kept down on the flats around the loch. They were lovely solid, shaggy creatures with gentle eyes and incongruously fierce horns. Corran was making silage to feed them in the winter, and in between work on the cottages kept up running repairs on gates and fences around the estate.

Lotty liked seeing him around the farm on

his tractor. She watched him studying his cattle, striding up a hillside or neatly stacking bales of silage, and felt a strange constriction in her chest. He looked so contained, so utterly at home here. You could tell just by looking at him that Corran McKenna didn't need anyone or anything else.

He seemed to be able to turn his hand to anything. In the cottages, he knocked down walls, plumbed in new bathrooms and kitchens, mended floorboards, made a new banister. 'How did you learn to do all this?' she asked him, watching him fit a shower in the first cottage.

Corran shrugged. 'I picked up a few skills in the Army. Here, hold this, will you?' He passed her a plastic door while he ripped open a packet of nuts and bolts with his teeth.

'You installed showers in the Army?'

'It was more about learning to do whatever needed to be done.'

Doing whatever needed to be done. Oddly, his comment reminded Lotty of her grandmother's steely resolve.

'Do you miss it?'

'The Army?' He shook his head as he took the door from her and manoeuvred it into position.

'No. It suited me for a while. After I graduated, all I wanted to do was be here—the one place I wasn't welcome. I was rootless and restless, and the Army gave me the challenge I needed, but I was too much of a loner to do well.' He glanced at Lotty. 'I'm not good at taking orders.'

'A bit of a drawback in the military,' she commented dryly, and the corner of his mouth lifted.

'You could say that. I was up for insubordination too often, but I had just as many citations after successful operations, and I got a reputation as a maverick. When my commission was up, I don't think the Army was that sorry to see me go.'

He screwed in the first bolt with a few deft twists of the screwdriver. 'I'd seen enough dusty hellholes by then, anyway. I missed the hills.' He looked out of the bathroom window to where the hillside soared up from the loch. 'There are hills in Afghanistan, but they're not like these.'

Lotty's eyes rested on his profile. He had that toughness and competence that must have made him a good officer, but she could see that he might not have been a successful team leader. He had grown up a lonely little boy, rejected by his father. Not surprising then that he was more comfortable going his own way, relying on himself. Corran McKenna wasn't a man who would let himself need anyone else.

The thought made her sad.

'Did you come straight back to Mhoraigh?'

Corran fitted another screw. 'No. As far as I knew, my father was still intending to leave the estate to Andrew then. I decided that if I couldn't have Mhoraigh, I would buy my own place, and all I needed to do was earn enough money to get started. So I set up a security company in London with a mate of mine. Jeff did all the schmoozing—he's good at that stuff—and I dealt with the practicalities. I didn't like being in London but it was the best place to make money.'

In went the last screw. 'And then my father sent for me when he knew he was dying, and everything changed.'

'I can't imagine you in London,' said Lotty.

'I can't either now, but actually I spent quite a lot of time there one way or another. My mother is a city girl through and through—God knows how she ever got together with my father—and after she left him she took me to London. She's been there ever since, getting married and divorced on a regular basis. Every time I went home from school, it seemed she was living in a different house with a different man, always convinced that *this* was going to be the one.'

Corran shook his head at his mother's capacity for self-delusion as he stepped back and tested the shower door.

'You must have thought that you had found the one too, when you got married.' Remembering that she was supposed to be clearing up, Lotty bent for the dustpan and brush. She had been longing to find out more about his marriage, and she might not get a better opening.

For a moment she was afraid Corran wasn't going to answer. 'I'm sorry to disappoint you, but it wasn't that romantic,' he said in the end. 'We only got married because Ella told me she was pregnant.' He caught Lotty's startled look. 'She said she'd had food poisoning so she'd missed a pill. It happens.'

'I didn't realise you had a child,' she said.

'I don't. We'd barely tied the knot when it turned out that it was all a mistake.'

'A mistake?' Lotty was staring at him with those grey eyes that tugged at a chord deep in his belly and made it impossible to ignore her the way he wanted to. Her hair was tied up in that absurd scarf with the jaunty knots. He had found her another shirt as the first one was so filthy after two days that she had had no choice but to wash it. This one was a dark blue tartan. Corran had never thought of it particularly before, but on Lotty it looked wonderful. *Sexy.*

'Didn't she take a test?'

He forced his mind back to the conversation. 'I don't know,' he said, blowing out a breath. 'It was stupid of me not to ask for proof, but it never occurred to me that she would make up something like that.'

'Were you disappointed?'

'No. I hadn't thought about having a family, so it was all a bit of a relief.'

'And yet you married Ella straight away.'

Uncomfortable, Corran hunched a shoulder. 'She said she wouldn't consider a termination, and I had to accept my part in it. She didn't get pregnant by herself.'

'No,' Lotty agreed, 'but you didn't have to get married either. This is the twenty first century.

There are plenty of successful single parent families out there.'

'I know that.' A muscle started jumping in his jaw. Talking of his marriage always made Corran feel like a fool, and he wished he hadn't started telling Lotty about it. 'We could have lived separately. I just didn't like the idea of a child of mine being shuffled from one parent to the other and made to feel a nuisance to both.'

He stopped, appalled to hear the bitter undercurrent to his words. It seemed to sizzle in the air. Lotty would think he was talking about himself. She would think he was pathetic, and screwed up still about a childhood that was long past. Which he wasn't. He didn't believe in self-indulgent wallowing in the past. What was the point of dwelling on it? What was done, was done. His parents had done their best, and he had grown up and made his own life. No problem.

But Lotty wouldn't realise that. She had been standing there, her head tilted slightly to one side, the way she did when she was listening, and she would have heard that self-pity bursting through. *Made to feel a nuisance to both.* Why didn't he just burst into tears and be done with it?

'I don't think wanting to make life easier for a child is a bad reason to get married,' said Lotty after a moment.

Corran busied himself collecting all the packaging from the shower. 'Well, it's just as well there was no baby. Ella and I were a disaster together.'

'There must have been something between you,' Lotty objected.

'Sex,' he said bluntly. 'That's not enough to keep a marriage going. Ella was—is—gorgeous, but she's desperately needy, and I'm not well-equipped to deal with that. She wanted constant attention, and I was too busy trying to keep the company running to give it to her. When you've seen the aftermath of a roadside bomb or watched kids used as human shields, it's hard to care much about sending text messages or arranging little surprise treats. I just didn't have the patience to deal with Ella's neuroses. To be honest, it was a relief when I found out that she was having an affair with Jeff.'

Lotty's jaw dropped. 'With your *friend?*'

'Jeff was much more Ella's type. God knows why she wanted to marry me in the first place.'

'Apart from the sex?' There was an unusual

squeeze of lemon in Lotty's voice, and a tinge of colour along her cheekbones. For some reason that made Corran feel better.

'Apart from that,' he agreed gravely.

He propped the cardboard against the wall and balled up the plastic sheeting. 'As it turned out, it all worked out for the best. Ella would never have come up to Loch Mhoraigh. She's a city girl, like my mother. Things got complicated with Jeff, of course, and the business went down the pan, but I'd heard from my father by then and I didn't care as long as I could get to Mhoraigh. I agreed to an outrageous divorce settlement, which is why I'm so skint now.'

'That doesn't seem very fair,' said Lotty. 'She was the one having the affair.'

Corran shrugged. 'But she was probably right when she said I didn't pay her enough attention. Besides, it was my fault for choosing a woman who was as unsuitable as my mother,' he said, stuffing the plastic into a black bin liner. 'You'd think I would have known better.'

'You love your mother,' said Lotty with such certainty that his head came up and he stared at her.

'What makes you think that?'

'You're looking after a dog called Pookie, for a start.' She glanced at his mother's dog, who was stretched out in a patch of sunlight, his flanks twitching as he dreamed of chasing rabbits.

Corran sighed. 'It's very hard to say no to my mother,' he conceded. 'I love her, of course I do, but she's impossible. Frivolous, scatty, the attention span of a midge. Utterly unreliable. She drifts through life dispensing charm and kisses and leaving emotional and financial chaos in her wake.

'It never occurs to my mother that someone— usually me—has to clear up the mess she leaves behind her,' he said, jabbing the last piece of plastic into the bin bag. 'Which is why I can't now understand how I ever got involved with Ella in the first place. It should have been obvious that we were completely unsuited, just like my parents.'

'Sometimes opposites attract,' suggested Lotty, her eyes on the dustpan and brush she was using to sweep up sawdust. For some reason she was feeling dispirited.

'In bed perhaps,' said Corran, 'but I'm looking for someone who's in for the long haul now.

My mother was a disaster here, and Ella would have been too. My stepmother stayed, but it was her fancy ideas that proved the real drain on the estate. It would be nice to have some female company, sure, but I've learnt my lesson. Next time, I'm going to be pragmatic. I'm looking for a nice, sensible, practical woman who'll fit right in and be prepared to share my life here. I don't need glamour. I need someone who can drive a tractor and help with the lambing.'

'Why stick at that? Why not insist that she can cook too?' said Lotty waspishly. 'Then she can be really useful!'

'The kind of woman I'm looking for *will* be able to cook,' said Corran. 'That goes without saying.'

He was warning her off. Lotty was sure of it. Just in case she was getting ideas.

Well, she had got the message. Lotty liked to think of herself as sensible, but she suspected Corran wouldn't agree. She had done her best with the cleaning, but there was no denying the fact that her practical skills were limited. And she certainly wasn't a cook.

She wasn't at all the kind of woman Corran was interested in.

And, even if she was, Lotty reminded herself, she couldn't stay at Mhoraigh. *I'm looking for someone who's in for the long haul,* Corran had said. She was strictly short haul. Her allegiance was to Montluce. That was the life she had been born to. She might be loving this brief escape, but nothing altered the fact that her place was in her own country, with the people she had been brought up to serve, not in these wild hills with a grim-featured man who hadn't even believed she would last this week.

A divorced man who would never let anyone close to him.

He wasn't at all the kind of man she should be interested in, either.

Still, she couldn't help the way her heart jumped when Corran came into the cottage the next morning. He had changed out of his usual old cords and holey jumper and was wearing dark trousers and a jacket. His shirt was open at the collar, but Lotty spotted a tie rolled up in his pocket. He was obviously going to wait until the very last minute before he put that on.

'You look very smart,' she said.

Corran grimaced as he glanced down at himself.

'I thought I'd better brush up for the solicitor.' He looked around the room, which was still dingy and grubby, but transformed from earlier in the week, and his gaze came back to Lotty, who was on her knees cleaning the skirting boards. 'Are you going to be OK here on your own all day?'

'I'll be fine.' Lotty wrung out a cloth into the bucket. The water was already filthy. 'I've got Pookie to protect me.'

Corran snorted as he eyed the little dog, who was sitting next to her, looking like a soft toy with his bright eyes and ears cocked as if he was following the conversation.

'He's not what you'd call an intimidating guard dog,' he pointed out. 'Unless you get a burglar with a phobia about fluff, in which case he might come in handy, I suppose.'

'No burglar is going to be bothered to come all the way out here,' said Lotty. 'Besides, there's nothing to steal.'

That was true enough. Still, Corran couldn't help worrying.

And that made him cross. This was exactly what he had been afraid of when he first let Lotty stay.

Worrying about someone else. He didn't need it, he thought irritably.

He had known Lotty would be a distraction, but he couldn't have guessed just how great a one she would prove to be. He couldn't shake the image of Lotty in the bath. It was as if the curve of her throat, the slim shoulders, the delicate line of her clavicle were burned into his mind. He could still see the wet, pearly skin, the arms clutched over her breasts, her soft mouth open in shock, her eyes huge and startled.

If only he wasn't so *aware* of her all the time. Even when he was ripping up floorboards or knocking down walls, he could see Lotty, slender, eyes shining, smiling that smile that made something stir queerly inside him. He could still picture her wrinkling her nose at a mug of tea or chewing her lip as she studied a recipe.

Much as he would like to dismiss her as a pampered brat, Corran couldn't deny that she was a hard worker. There was a steely resilience to her that he hadn't recognised at first, a stubbornness to the way she lifted her chin and refused to give in. He had pushed her unfairly hard, Corran knew, but she hadn't uttered a word of complaint about the conditions. Corran didn't know anyone else who would have put up with so much.

'I'll go to the supermarket on the way back,' he told her. 'Is there anything else you want?'

Lotty sat back on her heels and wiped her forehead with the back of her arm. 'Proper coffee,' she said.

'You've already put that on the list. Three times. And we don't need coffee,' he said. 'We've got plenty of tea.'

Lotty made a face, and he grinned at her, a brief, flashing smile, before he turned for the door. 'I'll see you later,' he said. 'Work hard.'

Princess Charlotte was hardly ever alone. There was always a footman outside the door, a lady-in-waiting with letters to be answered, her private secretary to discuss visits, a maid to help her dress.

So Lotty didn't mind being left on her own at all. She hummed as she tackled the grime on the skirting boards and tried to forget about how Corran had looked when he smiled. The grin made him look younger, warmer, more attractive.

Much more attractive.

She wasn't supposed to be noticing that he was attractive, Lotty reminded herself crossly. Hadn't he already warned her off? And hadn't she already remembered that she would be going home to Montluce before too long, and that she had had quite enough new experiences to keep her going for a while?

Losing her virginity was just going to have to wait.

It would be a shame to spoil things. In spite of everything, she liked Corran. She liked the fact that he made no concessions to her. He might be rude, but she could be rude right back. She could say whatever came into her head, and Corran wouldn't mind at all. In an odd way, they were friends. Lotty had never felt as comfortable with anyone before, that was for sure. She didn't want to spoil that by making an unwelcome pass that would embarrass him and humiliate her.

It was enough that he had let her stay.

And that she had kept her part of the bargain too. If she could finish washing down the paintwork, the cottage would be ready for painting by the end of the day and she would have done what she had promised to do, Lotty reminded herself.

She should be thinking about *that,* not Corran's smile.

But she couldn't help the alarming dip of her stomach when Corran came back earlier than she had expected. He appeared in the doorway of the cottage bedroom, all austere angles and hard planes, and in spite of herself Lotty's pulse kicked up a notch.

Eyes narrowed critically, he looked around the room. The floorboards were swept, the walls bare, the paintwork dingy with age but clean.

'Not bad,' he said.

'Not bad?' Lotty echoed, because it was easier than thinking about how lean and hard and un-touchable he looked. How could she have even *thought* about trying to attract a man like Corran? He was too tough, too uncompromising, too dauntingly self-contained.

She rested her fists on her hips. 'Is that all you can say? *Not bad?'*

'What would you like me to say?'

'For a start, you could say, "I'm sorry, Lotty, you were right and I was quite wrong when I said you wouldn't be able to get the cottage ready for painting in a week."'

Something that might have been a smile hovered around Corran's mouth. 'All right, I was wrong about that. There, satisfied?'

'Not quite. You also have to say, "and I was completely wrong about you not lasting a day". In fact, you might as well admit that you're well on your way to losing that bet we made.'

'That was for a month,' he reminded her. 'A lot can happen in three weeks.'

Lotty put her nose in the air. 'Well, I hope you didn't spend too much money in Fort William today, because you're going to have to save to take me out for that dinner!'

The dent at the corner of Corran's mouth deepened. 'You're a long way from earning that dinner, but I will give you a night off cooking. I splashed out on a ready-made curry.'

Not having to prepare the meal meant that Lotty could linger in her bath that evening, and she made the most of it. She was getting sick of putting on the same thing every evening but, short of ringing the changes between a camisole and a silk vest, she didn't have much choice. On went the jeans, on went the raspberry pink cardigan that clashed so horribly with her red hair. She hadn't thought about that when she threw a few clothes into her rucksack before she set off on the walk. She hadn't thought it would matter what she wore in the evenings.

It didn't matter. It was just that it might be nice to look more… feminine, more desirable.

Catching herself sighing, Lotty gave herself a mental slap. Pushing her feet into pumps, she shrugged on the cardigan and went downstairs to the kitchen, where Corran was heating up the curry.

'Can I do anything to—'

She stopped. A spanking new cafetière sat in the middle of the kitchen table, a packet of freshly ground coffee propped against it.

'I only bought it because I'm sick of you moaning about the instant coffee,' said Corran before she could say anything.

Lotty couldn't believe it. 'You bought *coffee! Real coffee!* Oh, thank you!' Without thinking, she threw her arms around him and hugged him, but even before her hands touched that solid body, she knew she'd made a mistake.

A *big* mistake.

Now, instead of imagining, she knew that he

felt as hard and strong as he looked. She knew how safe he felt, how steady. She could feel the steady beat of his heart, smell clean cotton and clean skin and something that was just Corran.

And for one tiny moment, his arms closed around her and he held her against him. It was an instinctive response to her throwing herself at him, Lotty was sure, but it felt so good, she let herself hope foolishly that he would never let her go.

He did, of course. A beat, another, three, and then he snatched his arms from around her and stepped sharply back.

Mortified, Lotty flushed. 'Sorry, it was just… I'm so thrilled by the idea of real coffee.' It sounded lame, even to her.

Corran turned away to check on the rice. 'It doesn't take a lot to thrill you, does it?' he said.

There was just a hint of something that might have been strain in his voice, but Lotty was still too embarrassed at the way she had thrown herself at him to wonder too much at it. She was more concerned to make sure that Corran knew she hadn't meant anything by her hug. Keep it light, she told herself.

'You know me,' she said. 'Easily excited.'

Then she wished she hadn't said that. It sounded suggestive somehow.

There was an awkward pause. Lotty's hands were thrumming with the feel of him. Not knowing what to do with them, she hugged her arms together and moved away as casually as she could while she tried desperately to think of something to say to break the lengthening silence.

In the end it was Corran who broke it. 'So, how did you get on today? You weren't too lonely?'

'No. Well, a bit at lunchtime, maybe.'

She had sat on the beach with just Pookie for company. She had noticed the driftwood on the shingle, the birds that wheeled overhead, the colours of the hills across the loch, but it hadn't been the same without him.

Corran put the rice and curry on the table, and Lotty pulled out a chair and sat down, still self-conscious. Her grandmother would be ashamed of her. All those years of training to put everyone at their ease no matter the circumstances, and she couldn't think of a single thing to say!

The silence stretched uncomfortably again.

'Um…how long does it take to get to Glasgow from here?' Lotty blurted out at last.

Corran stiffened. 'Two or three hours.' He shot her a sharp glance. 'Why? Are you planning to leave?'

Leave? The thought had panic clawing at Lotty's spine. 'No! No,' she said again, more calmly. 'I'm just sick of wearing the same clothes every evening. I left a case in left luggage at the station in Glasgow and I wondered how hard it would be to go and get it on the bus. Always supposing you'd let me have a day off, of course!'

'I don't know about that,' Corran said. 'Days off? Next thing, you'll be wanting sick pay and holidays and bonuses!'

They were both trying too hard, but it was better than that awful tense silence.

'Just one little day off,' Lotty pretended to wheedle. 'I promise I won't lift my nose from the grindstone for a minute after that!'

'I *was* thinking of going down to Glasgow myself at some point,' he said after a moment. 'I'll need to furnish and equip the cottages as we get them ready. There are big stores where you can get cheap and cheery flat pack furniture.

You might as well come with me,' he told Lotty gruffly. 'We could pick up your case at the same time.'

'That sounds great. Thank you!'

'I can't spare the time for a while yet, though,' he warned. 'If you're desperate, you'd better buy yourself something in Fort William. You can do the shop next week. Don't expect any fancy shops, though.'

Lotty parked Corran's Land Rover and reminded herself to lock it and put the key away safely. There was no footman here to drive the car away for her, to wash it and valet it and make sure that it was full of fuel before the next time she went out. All she normally had to do was get out and walk up the steps to the palace.

It was all very different here.

Lotty was excited at the trip to Fort William on her own. This was another whole new experience for her. She had been thrilled when Corran had told her she could do the supermarket shop. That morning he had handed her a wodge of cash.

'That'll have to be enough,' he said, and then he added some more notes. 'And this is for you.'

'For me?'

'Your housekeeping wages,' he explained patiently. 'It's not much, but you've earned it.'

Now that money was burning a hole in Lotty's pocket, and she was looking forward to her day off.

Not that she wasn't enjoying her job. Having cleaned the cottage from top to bottom, she had helped Corran do some minor repairs—filling in holes in the plaster, fixing the broken banister, replacing the kitchen window—and since then she had been painting. Lotty loved seeing how the cottage looked brighter and fresher with every stroke of the brush.

She was on her mettle about the cooking now too. Which was nothing to do with the fact that Corran was looking for a woman who could cook, because she didn't care, did she? And there was no point in trying to impress him. Still, Lotty wanted to do better, and she thought she was improving.

A little, anyway.

Now she felt as if she had earned her morning off. As Corran had warned, the shops were far from fancy, but Lotty didn't care. She shopped in Paris and London, but none of the very expensive designer shops she usually frequented compared to the fun of flicking anonymously through the racks in a cheap and cheerful chain store with the music thumping and a sales assistant filing her nails behind the counter and nobody paying the slightest bit of attention.

Lotty loved it.

She bought a couple of vest tops, a shirt and a cotton jumper and smiled to herself imagining her grandmother's expression. The Dowager Blanche would be horrified by the idea of her granddaughter in cheap off-the-peg clothes, and yet Lotty had more satisfaction buying them with the money she had earned from Corran than she had ever had buying designer labels with her inheritance.

CHAPTER FIVE

THINKING of her grandmother reminded Lotty that she ought to check in with Caro and make sure that everything was all right in Montluce. She wandered around until she found an internet café and sat down at a computer with a coffee.

Caro had written a long, chatty email, and made Lotty laugh describing her first meeting with the Dowager Blanche, and her grandmother's beloved pug. It was strange reading her friend's reaction to the palace and to Philippe, but she sounded in fine form, which was a big relief to Lotty, who had known just what a big deal it was when she had asked Caro to stand in as Philippe's girlfriend.

The Dowager Blanche had been intent on making a match between Lotty and Philippe ever since his father had become Crown Prince of Montluce, and Caro had agreed to act as a decoy while Lotty escaped. She had told her grandmother that she was too embarrassed to stay in

Montluce with Philippe flaunting his new girl-friend, which hadn't predisposed the Dowager Blanche to like Caro very much. Knowing how intimidating her grandmother could be, Lotty hoped she hadn't been too caustic to Caro. But Caro had obviously taken it all in good spirits, and was even generous enough to feel sorry for the Dowager.

I think that beneath all the guff about duty and responsibility and behaving like a princess, she's really worried about you, Caro had written.

Lotty sighed. She knew that Caro was right. Her grandmother had controlled every aspect of her life since her mother had died—and probably before then, knowing the Dowager. She was a small, erect woman with a rigid composure and an excoriating tongue. Everyone in Montluce re-spected and adored her in equal measure.

Lotty felt much the same. She knew her grand-mother loved her, but the Dowager didn't believe in open displays of affection. Lotty had not been allowed to run around and behave like other chil-dren. For as long as she could remember, she had been good and done what was expected of her.

Other members of the royal family, like Philippe,

had escaped, refusing to be crushed under the burden of duty and privilege, but Lotty had never dared stand up to her grandmother.

Until now.

Lotty drafted a careful email to the Dowager's private secretary, saying that she was safe and well, and another to Caro, telling her about what she'd been doing. Caro would laugh at the idea of her peeling potatoes or making tea, but Lotty was still loving it. She wasn't ready to go back to being dutiful just yet.

It was hard to shake off a lifetime of being good, though, and Lotty couldn't help feeling selfish and guilty as she drove back to Loch Mhoraigh House that afternoon. She had had such a lovely time pushing a supermarket trolley along the aisles. Even queuing to buy cheese from the delicatessen counter was fun. Lotty had never queued before, and it was a thrill to take a ticket and wait for her number to be called like everyone else.

On the way home, she stopped in the village to buy the basic items she could get at the shop there. Corran always shrugged off any suggestion that he try and improve his relationship with the community, claiming that he had more important things to do, but Lotty thought it was a shame. The least they could do was support the local shop, she said. He was lucky to have one so close.

Not that the shop offered a big range of stock. It had a post office counter at the back, and a small selection of basic goods. A plump woman with tightly permed grey hair and winged glasses presided behind the counter. She eyed Lotty with interest as she carried over milk and butter.

'You'll be working up at the big house?'

Unused to the way information travelled in village communities, Lotty was amazed. 'How did you know?'

'That's Corran McKenna's Land Rover you're driving,' she said, which was a pretty big clue when Lotty thought about it. 'Besides,' she went on as she rang up the milk and butter, 'they said at the hotel that you'd gone up there. We'd all expected to see you back before now.'

'No, I like it there,' said Lotty. 'I'm hoping to stay a couple of months. Corran's doing a great job,' she added loyally.

'Aye, well, his heart was always there, even as a wee boy.'

'Oh, you know him?'

'I did. I was Cook up at the big house for a while.'

'You're Mrs McPherson?' said Lotty in delight.

'I am.'

'Corran told me about your scones.'

Mrs McPherson flushed with pleasure and settled herself more comfortably against the counter. 'I used to make them for him specially,' she confided. 'I felt sorry for the lad. It was shameful the way they treated him, it was. I'm not saying he was an easy boy, but that child practically brought himself up. His father had no time for him, and his mother never cared what anyone thought of her. What a minx *she* was!' She sniffed disapprovingly. 'She was English, you know.'

Then she paused, evidently realising what she had said. 'Of course, not like *you*.'

Lotty couldn't help smiling at her discomfiture. 'I'm not English,' she reassured her.

'Is that so? You sound English.'

'That's because I went to school in England. I'm actually from Montluce.'

She waited to be told that Montluce was part of France but, to her consternation, it turned out that

Betty McPherson was an avid reader of gossip magazines, and knew all about Lotty's country and the crisis in finding a successor to her father.

'What a time that poor family has had!' she said, shaking her head.

'Yes, it's been difficult for them,' said Lotty, beginning to wish that she had kept her mouth shut. But she couldn't bring herself to deny her own country.

Mrs McPherson seemed to have followed the crisis in such detail that Lotty had a few moments' anxiety in case she was recognised, but the older woman didn't seem to have made the connection between the elegant Princess Charlotte and the scruffily dressed girl who stood in front of her. It was partly a question of expectation, Lotty knew, but she was glad that she had had her hair cut nonetheless, and perhaps the red hadn't been such a bad idea after all.

As soon as she could, she changed the subject by asking for Mrs McPherson's scone recipe. Her first attempt to make scones had been a disaster and left the kitchen full of smoke. Fortunately, this proved to be an effective diversion, and it was some time before she was able to escape, sent on her way with lengthy instructions.

'And don't forget to dust the baking tray with flour,' was Mrs McPherson's parting shot, which meant nothing to Lotty. She smiled anyway and waved from the door, hoping that she was going to be able to remember it all.

As soon as she got back to Loch Mhoraigh House, she rushed into the kitchen and tried to put Mrs McPherson's instructions into effect, but if anything that batch of scones were worse than the ones she'd made before.

And that was saying something.

'It doesn't matter,' said Corran, but Lotty wouldn't give up. How hard could it be to make scones?

Mrs McPherson made it sound so easy. The recipe books made it sound easy. So why couldn't she do it? Was she really so lacking in any talent or ability? The more she thought about it, the more depressed Lotty got.

What, really, was she good for? Smiling and shaking hands. That was it. She was going to have to go home to Montluce and all she would have to show for it would be some broken fingernails. Yes, she had acquired a few basic skills like peeling a potato or painting a wall, but neither was exactly challenging. Lotty was terribly afraid that when it came down to it, she was just the pampered princess that the anti-royalists thought her after all. A smiling face. A walking clothes hanger. Nothing more than that.

What if that was all she was?

Raoul the Wolf would be ashamed of her.

Lotty kept thinking about her grandmother, whose spine of steel never bent, who would never, ever admit that a member of the royal house of Montluce was beaten.

So she kept on making scones, as if that would prove something, although whether it was to her grandmother or herself or her illustrious ancestors Lotty was never quite clear.

And the scones kept turning out flat and hard.

'I really don't understand why it matters so much,' said Corran, as Lotty gazed despondently at that day's flat offering.

'I just want to be able to do something well,' she tried to explain.

'You do lots of things well,' said Corran impatiently.

'Like what?'

He hesitated. 'See?' she pounced on him. 'You

can't think of anything!' Her face crumpled. 'I'm useless!'

'You're not useless. What a ridiculous thing to say!'

Corran glowered at her. He wanted to tell her how she had changed the feel of the house just by being there. How he looked forward to coming in at the end of a long day and seeing her at the range, stirring some sauce with a dubious expression. How she lit up a gloomy day with her smile.

But he didn't know how to say it without making it sound as if he wanted her. Which he didn't.

Much.

Lotty was the last kind of woman he wanted to get involved with, Corran had to remind himself every day after yet another night haunted by the image of her in the bath. The pure line of her throat seemed to be etched into his brain and, no matter how hard he tried not to look, his eyes would catch on the sweet curve of her mouth.

She worked with a steely determination that would put many men far stronger than her to shame, but she was beautiful and, even tired and dirty and despondent, there was a glamour to Lotty that made Corran leery.

There was no place for glamour at Loch Mhoraigh House. His own mother had been a perfect example of how disastrous it could be when you took someone out of their natural milieu, and his brief marriage to Ella had simply underscored that. Corran wasn't making that mistake again. When he had time for a relationship again, it would be with someone who belonged here, someone who could offer practical support and do more than look decorative.

Already he was getting too used to having Lotty around. It made Corran uneasy. 'You're just looking for attention,' he told her crossly.

'You can't think of anything, can you?'

Corran could feel himself being driven into a corner. 'You're good with Pookie,' he offered at last.

It was true too. With Lotty to shower attention on him, Pookie had settled down and wasn't nearly as irritating. He still looked more like a toy than a dog, but he could be appealing enough when he tried. Sometimes when he sat on the sofa Pookie lay beside him on his back to have his tummy scratched and Corran found himself obliging.

Lotty was looking unconvinced. 'And you're a

whizz with a broom,' he tried again, but the face she made at him showed what she thought of that as an accomplishment.

'Those sausages you cooked yesterday were pretty good.'

'They were burnt!'

'I read somewhere that charcoal is good for you.'

A tiny smile quivered at the corner of her mouth. 'You're just trying to indulge me.'

'I'll do whatever it takes to get a meal on the table,' he said acidly. 'What gastronomic treat do we have tonight?'

'Mince again. It's all we've got left,' she added, seeing Corran's involuntary grimace. They had been eating a lot of mince recently. It was one of the few things she had learnt to cook without burning and even Corran was getting sick of it.

'We'll stock up again tomorrow on the way back from Glasgow,' he said. 'We can collect your case, buy some furniture and do a supermarket session on the way home. If we've got to waste a day, we may as well do everything at once.'

'What do you mean, you haven't got the code?' Corran looked at Lotty in exasperation. They were standing in front of the left luggage lockers, which were cleverly locked with a digital code.

'It was printed on a bit of paper and I put it in my purse to keep it safe.'

'The same purse you left on a pub table?'

She nodded guiltily. 'I'd forgotten all about it until we got here. I'm really sorry it's a wasted journey.'

'You can't be the only idiot who loses the code. We're not leaving here without that case,' Corran said. 'Stay there,' he ordered and strode off.

Lotty wasn't at all surprised to see him come back with a station official a few minutes later. He might not be able to lay on the charm, but he was competent. If something needed to be done, you could rely on Corran to do it.

She clearly wasn't required to do anything more than stand and look helpless, which wasn't hard, while Corran told the official how stupid and careless she had been. She did her best to seem crushed, but the truth was that she loved being ticked off.

'You might at least have the decency to look ashamed,' Corran said, not fooled by her downcast expression. 'Look at all the trouble you've put this poor man to—not to mention the trouble you've put *me* to!'

Lotty hung her head. 'You're right. I'm really sorry.'

Corran looked at her suspiciously but she tucked in the corners of her mouth and kept her lips firmly pressed together until her case was safely retrieved, at which point she offered the official a dazzling smile.

'Thank you so much.'

'There's no need to lay it on with a trowel,' Corran muttered, carrying her case in one hand and steering Lotty out of the station with the other.

'Trowel?' she echoed, puzzled.

'You know what I mean. Smiling at that poor man, making those big eyes at him…'

Lotty stared at him. 'I thought you wanted me to thank him?'

'A simple thank you would have been fine. You didn't need to fawn over him.'

'You know you're being completely unreasonable, don't you?'

'I'm just saying.'

'I would thank *you* too if you weren't being so crabby.' Lotty slid a glance at him under her lashes. 'Seriously, thank you, Corran,' she said after a moment. 'It means a lot to have my case back.'

'You didn't need me,' he said grouchily. 'All you had to do was smile at that man and he'd have opened every locker in the place for you.'

If she didn't know better, Lotty might even have thought he was jealous.

'I couldn't have done it without you,' she said, and was afraid that it was true.

Her case safely stowed in the back of the Land Rover, they then spent a trying afternoon buying furniture.

Corran was not a good shopper. The store was a cavernous warehouse with a complicated system of ordering by codes, and he was too impatient to take any interest in the process. 'God, what a nightmare,' he said, rubbing a hand over his hair. 'Let's do this quickly and get out.'

To everyone else they must have looked like any of the other couples there, Lotty thought. She found herself watching them wistfully, wondering what it would be like to be choosing furniture for your first home with someone you were planning to spend the rest of your life with. How much more fun than moving into palace apartments furnished with priceless antiques and every comfort you could possibly imagine, none of which you had chosen yourself.

She suppressed a sigh. A second glance would certainly have convinced anyone watching that she and Corran weren't like everyone else. They didn't touch each other, or confer with their heads together. Instead, Corran marched through the store, determined to get the job done as quickly as possible.

'A chair is a chair,' he said briskly, scribbling down the code for the first armchair he came across.

Lotty looked at him in disbelief. 'That'll look awful in the cottage,' she protested. 'It's absolutely horrible.'

'It's a holiday let. Nobody's going to care what they sit on.'

'*I* care,' said Lotty firmly. 'I haven't done all that painting for you to spoil everything with horrible furniture! You want the cottages to look simple and stylish, not cheap and nasty. If you're going to charge people to stay, it's the least they're going to expect.'

'Oh, very well,' Corran grumbled, scratching out the code. '*You* choose, then.'

So it was Lotty who picked out beds and chests and a table and chairs, and a simple colourful sofa for the living room. She added bedding and towels, lamps and tablecloths, and a complete set of kitchen equipment to the list, before handing it back to Corran to go and pay for it all.

He squinted at it. 'Are you sure we need all this stuff?'

'If you're advertising a furnished cottage, you're going to have to furnish it,' Lotty pointed out crisply.

And it was Lotty who charmed the assistant into arranging a separate delivery so that they left with just a brightly checked cloth for the kitchen table in Loch Mhoraigh House. 'Haven't we spent enough money?' he grumbled when Lotty picked it up.

'A few pounds isn't going to make much difference after all you've spent on the cottages,' she said. 'The kitchen is so bare at the moment. A cloth will make it look more welcoming.'

'Welcoming for who?' demanded Corran, tucking the credit card receipt away in his wallet. 'We're the only people who ever see the kitchen.'

'It's a shame. It's a lovely house,' said Lotty, who was still saddened by the echoing rooms and the bare patches where pictures had clearly been hanging on the walls for generations. 'It needs a lot of love.'

'It needs a lot of money,' said Corran, holding open the door for her as they headed out to the car park. 'Money I don't have at the moment. Once the cottages are up and running, I'm going to invite some financial types to come and have a look, see what we've done. If they're impressed and can see some potential, I'm hoping they'll consider investing in the estate as a whole, but the house is way down my priority list. I need new breeding stock, not tablecloths!'

'I can see that,' said Lotty, 'but I still think it's a pity the house isn't more comfortable. It wouldn't take much to make it nice, and then you could invite people round.'

'What people?' asked Corran sarcastically. 'No one from the village will set foot in Loch Mhoraigh House while I'm there.'

'Have you asked them?'

Corran's lips tightened as he opened the passenger door of the Land Rover for her. 'We've been through this, Lotty,' he reminded her shortly. 'I haven't got time to sit around being social. I don't care if the entire village is queuing up to be invited in.'

Lotty wasn't ready to let it go. 'You should be part of the community,' she said stubbornly. 'Quite apart from anything else, how are you going to meet that sensible wife when you're a recluse?'

'I'm not a recluse.' Irritation gave Corran's tone a sharp edge. 'I'm just busy at the moment. And I've certainly got no money to spend tarting up the house for non-existent visitors!'

Lotty held the bright tablecloth on her knees. She hated the thought that the village distrusted Corran so much. If they could just meet him and get to know him, she was sure they would realise that he wasn't the monster his brother seemed to have painted him.

'I hope you'll get round to it one day,' she said as Corran started the engine. 'I'd like to think of the house brought back to life as well as the cottages. It must have been wonderful in its heyday. It's the kind of house that should be full of people, and have lots of children and dogs running around,' she added wistfully.

'Well, I've got the dogs,' said Corran. 'If you can count Pookie as a dog!'

He threw an arm along the back of Lotty's seat as he put the Land Rover into reverse and swung round to look over his shoulder. Lotty was very conscious of his hand near her shoulder. If he lifted it just a little bit, he could caress her neck.

If he wanted to.

Which he didn't.

She swallowed.

'I think you'll miss Pookie when your mother gets back,' she said. 'I've seen the way you tickle his tummy sometimes when you think I'm not looking! Under that tough exterior, you're just a softie.'

Corran finished manoeuvring out of the tight parking space before he glanced at Lotty. 'I only do that to shut him up,' he said, but there was a definite hint of a smile around his mouth all the same.

How did he do that, smile and not smile at the same time? It made Lotty feel very strange. One look at his mouth doing that not-quite-smiling thing, and she ended up feeling hollow and light-headed and sort of...*fizzy*.

She made herself look away.

'Anyway,' Corran went on, fortunately unaware of her reaction, 'the chances are that my mother will have forgotten all about Pookie by the time she gets home. She'll have moved on to some new enthusiasm, and it'll be, *Oh, darling, I'm sure he'd be so much happier if he stayed with you.* And then I'll be stuck with him!' Corran shook his head. 'Another ten years or so of calling a dog Pookie! Meg won't be able to hold her head up with the shame of it! At least she's a proper dog, who can bring the sheep in off the hill. What's Pookie good for?'

'He's a companion,' Lotty managed.

'I don't need a companion,' he said. 'I need a dog who's some use to me.'

Just like he needed a wife who was some use to him, thought Lotty sadly.

Corran moved the gear lever into first. Now his hand was near her knee. The same hand that could have stroked her neck, if only he had moved it just a little.

Lotty wrenched her eyes away from it. Her

mouth was dry. The Land Rover felt as if it had shrunk since they had driven down to Glasgow that morning. Now the sides were pressing in around her, pushing all the spare oxygen out of the vehicle and making the air twang under the pressure.

Nothing had changed, Lotty told herself. She was the same, Corran was the same, the Land Rover was the same.

She had spent too much time watching all those couples, that was all. It had made her twitchy. All that time she had spent reminding herself to be cool and careful around Corran, and now she might as well not have bothered. She was agonisingly aware of him beside her, and she shifted in her seat, desperate to find a way to convince him—or herself—that her heart wasn't pounding and her throat wasn't tight. Everything was just the same.

'The children will love Pookie,' she made herself say.

Corran stared at her. 'What children?'

'Well… I presume you're thinking of having a family?'

'I'm not married yet!'

'Loch Mhoraigh would be a lovely place to bring up children,' Lotty persevered, not even sure why she was making such a big deal of it. 'You should have lots, and make sure their childhood isn't like yours.'

Corran swung the Land Rover into the main road and put his foot on the accelerator. 'I haven't got time for any of that,' he said briskly. 'I've got the cottages to finish, an estate to get back on its feet, and then—maybe!—I can turn my attention to the house and finding another wife. It'll be time enough then to talk about having children,' he said. 'That's years down the line! Having a child now would be a disaster, just like it was for my parents. I've got far more important things to think about before then.'

'Like what?'

'Like getting new breeding stock, improving my herds. I need to buy some good rams in October.'

'I've hardly seen any sheep,' Lotty realised.

'That's because they're all up on the hills at the moment. You'll see plenty come September when we take the sheep to market,' said Corran.

But in September she would be gone. 'I'd like to

see that,' Lotty said in a level voice, 'but I won't be here then.'

She looked out of the window, suddenly bleak. In September she would be back in Montluce, back to her life as Princess Charlotte, always good, always obliging. A princess who never behaved badly. Who never sulked or lost her temper or felt herself burning up with desire.

And Corran would be here, taking his sheep to market, Meg at his heels and Pookie under his feet, bringing the estate back to life, without her.

Perhaps it would all be for the best. If her grandmother finally gave up the idea of her marrying Philippe, Lotty might be allowed to meet someone else. There had to be some prince or count somewhere the Dowager Blanche would deem a suitable match. Someone who understood royal life, who would know how to behave and how to smile and shake hands, who would be a dignified consort for Princess Charlotte of Montluce. Then Lotty could be married and lose her tiresome virginity to her husband. It would be sweet. It would be safe. It would be sensible.

But Lotty didn't want sweet and sensible. She didn't want suitable. She didn't even want safe.

Not yet.

This might be the only chance she ever had to be reckless, her only chance to take what she wanted without worrying about what the papers might say, or how her grandmother would react.

All those ancestors had had a chance to live dangerously, one way or another. Why not her?

A little fling, a brief affair… Was that so much to ask for?

Absently Lotty rubbed her thumb over her poor, cracked fingernails and allowed herself to revisit the question that had been simmering at the back of her mind ever since that first bath at Loch Mhoraigh.

Why not ask Corran?

Under her lashes, she watched Corran driving with the same cool competence he did everything else. The long, solid body was relaxed, his eyes narrowed, the big hands very sure on the wheel. The flex of muscles in his thigh when he braked sent such a surge of lust through her that she was dizzy with it.

It wasn't as if Corran was involved with anyone else. He was a free agent, and so was she.

So why not?

Of course, she wasn't Corran's type. He'd made it clear that he was looking for quite a different kind of woman, but that just made it better, didn't it? There would be no problem about her leaving after a couple of months. She could say goodbye and he would never know who she really was. Not that Lotty thought Corran was the kind of man who would tattle to the tabloids, but who knew really? *How I seduced virgin princess* was a story some papers would pay a lot of money for, and the Mhoraigh estate was badly in need of cash.

Besides, she didn't want him to know she was a princess. She wanted him to think of her as an ordinary girl. She wanted him to make love to her as an ordinary girl. She couldn't bear it if he suddenly started treating her carefully. No, she wouldn't tell him, ever.

He was single, attractive, and they were alone together most of the time. If she wanted to lose her virginity, Lotty thought, she might never have a better chance.

Why *not* Corran?

The sensible side of Lotty, the side that wasn't giddy with desire, pointed out that she had no idea how to go about seducing a man and that, even if she did, Corran wasn't the kind of man who would fall for any tricks. There was something dauntingly unflirtable about him. She simply wouldn't dare.

So there was no point in thinking about it any more.

Only that didn't stop her nerves crisping every time Corran reached for the gearstick between them. Every time he shifted his hands on the wheel or flicked a glance up at the rear view mirror, she found herself sucking in her breath. And every time she would wonder what it would be like if she *did* dare ask him to be her lover.

Because then she would be able to put her hand on that long, tantalising thigh. She would be able to look at the uncompromising line of his jaw without feeling sick with longing.

She would know what it felt like to press her lips to his throat. She would know the hard planes of his body, the shift of his muscles, the touch of his hands.

Lotty began to feel feverish. Fixing her eyes desperately on the road ahead, she swallowed and twisted her fingers together.

'Are you all right?'

Corran's abrupt question made her jump. 'Fine,' she said brightly. Too brightly. 'Absolutely fine.'

'You're very quiet.'

'Am I? I suppose I was just thinking about going home.'

'It's not much further,' said Corran. 'Another hour, maybe.'

'No, I meant home to Montluce.'

There was a pause. 'Oh. Yes, of course.' The silence lengthened uncomfortably. Corran cleared his throat. 'I don't know anything about your country. What's it like there?'

Lotty looked out of the window, remembering her home. 'Everything's on a small scale in Montluce. It's like a fairy tale country in lots of ways. Mountains, lakes, castles, little old towns. It's pretty.'

Her eyes rested on the great sweeps of hillside, their starkness softened and turned to gold in the early evening sun. 'Here, it's…wilder. Grander somehow.' A sigh escaped her. 'I'm going to miss it.'

'Do you have to go?' Corran asked. He wasn't looking at her. He was looking at the road ahead, and it sounded to Lotty as if the question had been forced out of him.

'Yes,' she said on a breath. 'Yes, I do.'

Three months, she had agreed with Philippe, who was only standing in as regent while his father, the Crown Prince, was recovering from a major illness. The moment his father was better, Philippe would be leaving Montluce, he had told Lotty frankly, and that meant the country would need a first lady once more. Who better than Princess Charlotte, who had spent years doing the job for her own father? She had the perfect combination of warmth and dignity. The people loved her.

Ever since she was a child, Lotty had had the importance of duty and responsibility dinned into her. Her grandmother hadn't hesitated to point out that Lotty would be monumentally selfish if she insisted on her own life after her father had died. How could she even think about refusing and letting the new Crown Prince down? How could she think about letting her *country* down?

She couldn't. This was the only rebellion Lotty could allow herself.

'I have to go back,' she said. 'I don't have a choice.'

'But not yet?'

Was that a hint of anxiety in his voice? Lotty swivelled in her seat to look at him, longing to believe that it was true. His eyes were flickering between road and mirrors, but his jaw was set. She could see the tension jumping in his cheek.

'No,' she said slowly, 'not yet.'

CHAPTER SIX

THREE months, Lotty had given herself. She had been here for three weeks already…was she going to make the rest of the remaining time?

It was all very well deciding to do something about the lust that had her in its grip, but how exactly was she going to go about it? Lotty squirmed in her seat, mentally rehearsing scenes.

Should she just grab Corran once they got back to the house and hope he got the idea? She couldn't see herself having the nerve to do that, descendant of Raoul the Wolf or not.

Or she could lead up to the question in a diplomatic fashion. *I was wondering what your views were on brief flings?* she could ask him, and then if he said that he was all for them, that would give her an opening at least.

Or perhaps she should be grown up and discuss the matter openly as two consenting adults.

Yes, grown-up was good, but the more Lotty

tried to think about how such a conversation might go, the deeper she lost herself in a morass of euphemisms. Perhaps the grabbing option wasn't such a bad one, after all.

One thing became clear to Lotty during that interminable drive. It had been a mistake to bottle up the physical attraction she felt. Something about being shut up in the Land Rover with Corran for so long seemed to have acted as a pressure cooker, and choosing furniture together had merely lifted the lid on her feelings, which were now threatening to explode out of control.

Lotty was alarmed by the way her hands were twitching and she had to clutch them together in her lap in case they wandered over to Corran of their own accord. She felt physically ill: giddy and slightly nauseous, her heart pounding, her throat dry. Was it normal to believe that the only way she could ever feel better again was if she could touch him?

If only she had more experience, she would know what to do. Was the chance of being able to coil herself around him and press her mouth to that pulse beating in his throat worth the risk of making a monumental fool of herself? Lotty couldn't decide. She couldn't think. She could just sit there and give up on the idea of pretending that she didn't want him, while the air in the Land Rover grew tauter and tauter with every mile.

When they drew up in the stable yard behind Loch Mhoraigh House, Lotty practically threw herself out of the Land Rover to gulp at the fresh air, only to find that her legs were so weak that she had to hang on to the door.

Perhaps she really *was* ill?

Lotty told herself to get a grip. She was distracted for a little while by unpacking the shopping, and she made herself breathe deeply: in, out, in, out. Not too difficult once you had got the hang of it. She was very glad Corran had left her to it while he took the dogs out. Pookie was thoroughly overexcited after being left all day.

'I've put your case upstairs,' Corran said briefly before he left.

She would be able to change into something decent for a change. Lotty clung to the hope that wearing clothes from her old life would remind her that she was a princess, not a skittish, fevereyed girl in a frenzy of lust. She would put on the clothes she wore in the palace, and she would miraculously become sensible and dignified again.

Only it didn't work out like that.

Lotty remembered packing her most casual clothes, but everything she pulled out of the case looked far too smart for Loch Mhoraigh House. She was half inclined to put it all back, but having made such a fuss about getting the suitcase back, it would look odd if she didn't wear anything from it.

She chose the most relaxed outfit she could find—a pair of loose trousers and a silk knit top, a scarf knotted casually at her throat—but, far from restoring her to her normal regal self, the slip of the luxurious materials against her skin only made her feel more edgy. Every cell in her body seemed to be jangling with awareness. She didn't know what to do with her hands, or her feet, and she couldn't settle to anything.

Corran was checking the oven but he glanced up briefly when Lotty went into the kitchen, and then did a double take. Closing the oven door, he straightened slowly.

'You look very elegant,' he said.

Elegant. It was a horrible word, Lotty decided.

It was cold and restrained. She didn't want to be elegant. She wanted to be foxy. She wanted to be sexy. She wanted to be *hot*.

And elegant didn't belong at Loch Mhoraigh either. Elegant was out of place, just like she was, Lotty thought miserably.

They had bought a ready meal to heat up for supper, but Lotty was too tense to enjoy the break from cooking. The soft trousers whispered against her legs whenever she shifted in her seat, and with every stretch of her arm, every lift of her hand, the silky top caressed her bare skin. She wished she had her old jeans and pink cardigan on again, or—even better—her filthy working clothes. Anything would be better than sitting there, simmering, unable to think about anything except her own body and Corran sitting across the table.

She was preternaturally aware of him, of his fingers holding the foil packet steady as he helped himself, of the broad, strong wrists. She couldn't risk looking into those iceberg eyes, but her gaze skittered around the rest of his face, from the dark brows to the forceful nose, across his cheek to his temple, along the uncompromising line of his jaw, and always back to his mouth.

That *mouth.*

Lotty's pulse was roaring in her ears. She couldn't believe that she had spent every other evening sitting at this same table, happily chatting to Corran. At least, she had chatted happily and Corran had offered caustic comments, but it had been comfortable.

It wasn't comfortable now.

How could one day have changed so much? It wasn't as if anything had happened. All they had done was sit in the Land Rover, and walk around two stores. And yet it felt as if a fault line had appeared between them, shifting the world out of kilter, and squeezing all the air out of the atmosphere. Lotty had years of experience of stilted situations. She knew just what to do to move the conversation on, to make people relax and smile.

But not now. She felt like a hot air balloon, precariously tethered, and it would take only one little tug and she would just float away out of control. It was all she could do to keep herself in her chair. So their lame attempts at conversation kept getting stuck while Lotty pushed her food around her plate.

'Not hungry?'

'Not really.'

'Me neither,' said Corran, pushing the plate aside. 'Let's go out.'

Lotty looked at him blankly. 'Out?'

'I'm stir crazy after a whole day indoors or in the car. I need some exercise. We could go for a walk.'

Lotty's heart was beating high and hard in her throat. 'OK.'

Outside, it was one of those long, soft Highland evenings she had come to love so much. Corran had told her it was a different story in winter, when the days were short and it was dark and bitterly cold, but in June the sun was only just setting at half past nine, and the cloudless sky was washed with an uncanny orange light.

The breeze ruffling the surface of the loch still carried the warmth of the day, but Lotty was hugging her arms together and her shoulders were hunched with tension.

'Cold?' Corran asked her. 'Do you want to go back and get a jacket?'

'No, I'm just… No, it's fine.' He could see her making an effort to relax her shoulders. 'I'm fine,' she said again, but she tucked her hair behind her ears in a gesture he had seen her make before when she was uncertain.

She had been tense all afternoon. Corran couldn't put his finger on when things had changed. She had been her usual self on the way down to Glasgow, but gradually the ease had leaked out of the air, and then she had started talking about going home.

Her home, which wasn't Loch Mhoraigh at all. Corran had been conscious of a nasty jolt at the reminder. Of course, he knew that Lotty wasn't going to be there permanently—that had been the deal, after all—but he hadn't thought she'd be thinking about going home yet.

He hadn't thought at all. He'd just got used to Lotty being there. She'd turned into a more useful worker than Corran would ever have imagined and between them they were making good progress on the cottages. Which would explain the rush of relief when she had said that she wasn't leaving immediately, of course.

Corran didn't want to think about an alternative explanation.

On the whole he was glad Lotty had reminded him that she was only there temporarily. For some reason she was making a point of it today. Corran almost hadn't recognised her when she came into the kitchen earlier. She was wearing trousers and a top, just as she had done every evening, but that outfit screamed sophistication and style. And money. Corran didn't know much about clothes, but even he could see that it must have cost a lot of money. He wondered how many rams he could have bought for the cost of that pair of trousers.

She looked different. Elegant, expensive, a creature from a different world. She made Ella's fashionable wardrobe look cheap. She didn't look like she belonged at Mhoraigh any more.

And that was a good thing, Corran tried to convince himself. It made it easier for him to ignore the way her mouth tilted when she smiled. Made it easier to pretend that the blood didn't rush to his head every time he looked into those luminous grey eyes.

She was walking beside him in silence, fiddling with the inevitable scarf at her neck, slender, straight-backed, those trousers swishing around her legs. Her face was averted slightly, and that meant he could let his eyes rest on the pure line of her throat as it swept down from her ear and curved into her shoulder. Sometimes Corran let himself imagine kissing his way down it…

He pushed the thought aside with a scowl. What was the point? Lotty was the last kind of woman he needed, Corran reminded himself. She didn't belong here any more than Ella would have done, any more than his mother had done. There was no point in imagining what it would be like to draw her close and taste that soft, sweet mouth, to gentle his hands down her spine and discover if her skin was as warm and smooth as it looked.

No point at all.

Corran didn't even know why he had suggested this walk. It was just reminding him how out of place Lotty was. And yet somehow she looked completely right here with the hills and the water. Somehow she *felt* right walking by his side.

Still thoroughly overexcited by their return, Pookie jumped around Meg, who did her best to ignore him as she trotted at Corran's heels. They walked past the beach where they had lunch, and on around the loch side until the track petered into a narrow deer path which led at last to a perfect curve of beach at the end of the loch. Behind, the hills soared up into the sky, while the loch stretched gleaming down the glen.

Lotty just stood and looked for a while. Then she drew a long breath. 'It's beautiful,' she said.

'I always think of this as my beach,' said Corran. 'I used to come here all the time. No one ever found me—not that they would ever have looked.'

He sat down on the ledge of tufty grass, stretching his legs out onto the shingle. After a moment, Lotty sat down beside him, close but not touching.

The spectacular light was fading slowly from orange to a purplish colour, but it wouldn't get properly dark until well after midnight. It was lovely to be out without the midges pestering and Lotty leant back on her hands and lifted her face to the breeze. She could hear it rustling over the grass, and the faint slap of the little waves ruffling the water.

And the boom of her pulse.

Corran was very close. He was looking out over the loch. Lotty could see the heart-wrenching line of his jaw and the very edge of his mouth. She wanted to tear her eyes away, but she couldn't. She couldn't stop thinking about how it would feel to touch him.

Then he turned his head and all the air left her lungs in a whoosh.

'You're very quiet,' he said. 'What are you thinking about?'

Lotty felt as if she were teetering on the edge of a cliff. If she stepped off, she could never step back.

She stepped anyway. Almost before she had thought of what she was going to say, she had opened her mouth and the words came out as if they had a will of their own.

'I'm wondering if I dare ask you to k-kiss me.'

There was a long, long silence, while her words echoed out over the water and rang up in the hills. *K-kiss me. K-kiss me. K-kiss me.*

'Do you?' said Corran at last.

'Do I what?' She could feel embarrassment prickling beneath her skin as the colour crept up her throat.

'Do you dare?'

Lotty drew a breath. 'What would you say if I did?'

A suspicion of a smile hovered at the edge of his mouth. 'I think I'd be able to oblige.'

'Oh.' The wretched colour deepened. This was when some darkness would help. She pulled at the grass beside her. 'The thing is…I should warn you…I've never had a boyfriend.'

It wasn't often she caught Corran by surprise, but he definitely blinked. 'What, never?'

'No.' She moistened her lips. She had started, so she might as well tell him it all. She couldn't be any more embarrassed anyway.

She went back to plucking at the grass, not looking at him. 'I'm a v-virgin. It's one of the reasons I wanted to have this time by myself. I know it can't last for ever, but I thought it would be a good opportunity to…to…lose my virginity,' she finished in a rush.

'It would just be a temporary thing,' she hurried on before Corran could speak. She was desperate to get it all out before she lost her nerve completely. 'I know I'm not your type. It's just…I wondered…' Moistening her lips, she took a determined breath. 'The thing is, I wanted a lover, only I wasn't sure how to go about finding one and I just wondered, well, I thought…'

'…that I would do?' Corran suggested when she ran out of steam.

But he didn't sound offended and, when Lotty risked a glance at him, she saw that the dent at the corner of his mouth had definitely deepened. Warmth bloomed deep inside her.

'Well, there isn't anyone else out here,' she pointed out, just so that he knew that she wasn't planning to get too involved.

'No, there isn't, is there?'

Reaching out, Corran ran an unhurried knuckle down Lotty's cheek, and her throat tightened at the tenderness of the gesture from the hard hand.

'Why don't we start with a kiss and take it from there?' he suggested.

'OK.' Lotty tucked her hair behind her ears and cleared her throat. Now that it had come to it, she was terrified and excited and very nervous that she wouldn't do it right.

'Don't tell me you haven't been kissed before either?'

'Not really.' How could she explain to Corran about the lonely pedestal she lived on, or how closely protected she had been by her grandmother all her life?

'Incredible,' he said, his eyes searching her face. 'Like a princess in a fairy tale, locked away, waiting for a kiss…'

Lotty's gaze slid from his. 'Something like that.'

Corran shook his head in disbelief as he laid his palm against her cheek. 'Are you going to ask me, then?'

The air was soft and sweet but Lotty shivered at his touch as he slid his hand down to her throat.

'Please would you kiss me?' she asked politely, and then he did smile. He really smiled, and something blossomed inside her. She had dreamt about seeing Corran smile like that, about seeing the hard mouth soften and the cold eyes warm, and the cheeks crease with amusement, and her heart contracted at the sight.

'Yes, I'll do that,' he said, but he still didn't kiss her. Instead he twisted his fingers around the scarf and drew it slowly from her throat. Lotty felt the coolness of the silk sliding over her skin and she closed her eyes, overwhelmed by the fizzy rush of anticipation and nervousness.

At last…at last!

Corran's lips touched the corner of her mouth, and her eyes flew open in dismay. 'Is that it?' she said, unable to keep the disappointment from her voice.

'No.' His smile deepened. 'That's not it. That's just the start. Come here,' he said, pulling her close so that he could trail tantalising kisses along her jaw to her earlobe and then down to the pulse that was beating frantically in her throat.

Lotty arched her head back instinctively and her fingers curled in the grass. His lips were so warm, so sure as they made their way back towards her mouth, and then he was torturing her with slow kisses on the other side. It was agonizing. It was wonderful. Lotty's senses were spinning with the wicked, delicious pleasure of it even as she burned with frustration.

And then his mouth reached hers at last, and the pleasure rocketed into a new urgency, a hunger that had her hands lifting instinctively to his shoulders so that she could hold on to him. His lips were warm and sure on hers, while his tongue teased until she parted her own and he took her with him as they sank down into the grass so he could kiss her in a way she'd only ever dreamed of before, long, long kisses, hungry but unhurried.

Lotty gave herself up to the sheer sensuous pleasure of it. Beneath her, the grass prickled her neck but she didn't care. She felt only the warm weight of Corran pressing her down into the ground, his hard hands sliding insistently over her thigh, slipping beneath her top to trace patterns of fire on her bare skin. It felt so good to be able to touch him too, to run her own hands over his back and feel the flex of his muscles beneath his shirt.

'I like this,' she gasped at one point, and Corran smiled against her skin.

'I can't believe you've never done this before,' he said.

'Am I doing it right?' she asked, suddenly uncertain, and he lifted his head to look down into her face, touched and amazed by her innocence. Lotty might be no expert, but she was so sweet and so eager and she felt so sinfully good.

'You're a natural,' he told her, and a smile lit the beautiful grey eyes.

'Really?'

'Really.'

'Would you kiss me again?'

'Why don't *you* kiss *me?*' Corran rolled onto his back and spread his arms. 'I'm all yours.'

Lotty smoothed her hair behind her ears, the

way she always did when she was nervous, but she leant over him and looked down into his face for a moment before lowering her mouth to his. She was tentative at first, a little unsure, but he lay still and let her discover just what she could do.

And she could do quite a lot. Corran had to clench his hands to stop his arms clamping around her and rolling her beneath him once more. He didn't want to frighten her, but she was sorely testing his control. She was lying right on top of him, tracing the angle of his cheekbones with light, butterfly kisses, kissing her way to his ear and then back to his mouth. Who would have thought that those sweet little kisses could be quite so tantalising, quite so sexy, quite so exciting?

When he couldn't take any more—and Corran thought he had done pretty well to last as long as he did—he brought his arms up and held her protectively while he eased her beneath him once more and kissed her hard, once, twice and a third time, more lingeringly, because he couldn't resist it.

'More,' said Lotty, winding her arms around his

neck when he tried to lift his head, so he kissed her again.

The kiss went on a long, long time, and Lotty abandoned herself to it until Corran levered himself away from her.

'I think it's time we went back,' he said unevenly.

'Oh,' said Lotty, disappointed. 'That's it? We're stopping?'

Corran pulled her to her feet and brushed the grass off her. 'We've only just got started,' he said.

'I don't understand,' Lotty said, but she let him take her hand and tug her back towards the house. 'Why do we have to go back?'

'There's the little matter of protection to think about,' Corran pointed out. 'I thought we were just having a walk. I didn't come prepared.'

'Protection?' Lotty's mind was reeling. She felt as if she were drugged with delight, and her whole body was humming with the feel of Corran's mouth on hers, his warm hands on her body.

When she thought of protection, she thought of her close protection officer, the one she had given the slip in Paris. She and Corran had been alone together for weeks. There was no one else around. Why would they need someone to protect them now?

Corran sighed. 'You do know where babies come from, don't you, Lotty? Even you can't be that innocent!'

'Oh,' said Lotty, finally making the connection. 'I didn't think of that,' she confessed.

'Besides,' he added, 'we'll be more comfortable in a bed.'

'Oh.' A shivery tide of anticipation and apprehension washed through Lotty. 'Oh,' she said again.

Afterwards, Lotty couldn't really remember walking back to the house. Wrapped in a strange dreamlike state, she had no idea if they had talked or not. All she remembered was the feel of Corran's strong fingers laced through her own, how warm and firm they had been.

They must have done something with the dogs when they got back, but she didn't remember that either. There was just Corran letting go of her hand at the door to his room.

'Are you sure, Lotty?' he asked. 'We can take it slow if you want.'

Lotty shook her head. 'No,' she said, stepping

up to him so that she could slip her arms around his waist and sucking in a breath at the taut solid strength of his body. 'I don't want to go slow,' she said. 'I'm sure.'

Lotty lay on her side so that she could watch Corran, who was splayed on his front over the bed. She didn't know how he could sleep. She was exhausted, but too overwhelmed to relax herself. She had known what happened in theory, of course, but she hadn't known it would be like *that*.

'Let go', Corran had said, and she had. It had been like flying, terrifying and exhilarating. Now every cell in her body was fizzing with satisfaction, but at the same time she felt shaky and uncertain. All her boundaries had shifted, and she couldn't go back to being the person she had been before.

But that was what she had wanted, wasn't it? She had wanted to know what everyone else seemed to have, and now she did. Lotty's lips curved at the memory. It had been a revelation—Corran's mouth, Corran's hands, his lean hard body, and how they could make her *feel*. Lotty burned at the memory.

She could look at him properly now that he was sleeping, and her eyes drifted wonderingly over the curve of his shoulder, the line of his back. His body was solid and male, with warm sleek skin. Who could have imagined that he would be a lover like that, that all that passion could be pent up behind the cool competence?

As if sensing her gaze, Corran stirred and rolled over, opening one eye as he encountered Lotty's warmth, and then the other. Lotty could see him remembering just what she was doing there.

'Good morning,' she said nervously. She hadn't been sure if she should slip back to her own room once he had fallen asleep. She had spent her whole life absorbing the correct protocol for different situations, but no one had ever told her the etiquette for sleeping with a man for the first time.

'Good morning,' said Corran. He shifted into a more comfortable position so that he could study her face. 'Are you OK?' he asked.

'I think so,' said Lotty. Given what they had done the night before, it was absurd to feel shy now, but her eyes slid away from his all the same. She looked at his shoulder instead. 'Corran, is it always like that?'

He reached out and tilted her chin up so that she had to look at him again. 'It's never going to be your first time again, Lotty, but it's only going to get better, I promise you that.'

What did that mean? Lotty regarded him doubtfully. 'Was I b-bad?' she asked, wincing inwardly at that betraying stutter.

Corran stretched, and Lotty caught her breath at the flex of his muscles and the sheer, unfamiliar maleness of him. 'Very,' he said.

Well, she shouldn't have asked the question if she didn't want to know the answer, Lotty reminded herself. She bit her lip. 'I did tell you that I wasn't experienced.'

'Lotty,' he said, exasperated, 'you were very bad in a very good way!' Sighing, he reached out and pulled her into the hard curve of his body. 'How is it someone so beautiful has so little belief in herself?'

What was there to believe in? Lotty wondered. She was a princess, and that was all anybody ever saw. She had never had a chance to be anything else, never had to prove herself. People treated her as special because of who she was, not because of what she was, Lotty had always known that.

Until now. Corran didn't know she was a princess. If he had known, would he have made love to her last night? Lotty didn't think so. They had been as intimate as two people could get, but he still didn't know the most important thing about her. Lotty didn't like the feeling that she was keeping a secret from him, especially now, but if she told him, he might change, and she couldn't bear that.

No, she wouldn't tell him yet.

Putting the flat of her hands on Corran's chest to hold him away slightly, she said, 'This won't change things between us, will it?'

'I would imagine it would, yes,' he said dryly.

'I don't want it to.'

'It's a bit late for that, Lotty.' Corran had been smoothing his hand possessively over the curves of her body but paused at that and a frown touched his eyes. 'I thought this was what you wanted.'

'It was,' she said. 'It's just that I want everything else to stay the same.'

He took his hand off her. 'Are you trying to say that you don't want to do this again?'

'No!' said Lotty, horrified. 'No, I do want that. Definitely.' Corran's expression was as hard to read as ever, and abruptly Lotty lost her nerve. 'If you didn't mind, of course.'

A smile quivered at the corner of his mouth as he pretended to consider the matter. 'I think I could bear it,' he said and put his hand back.

'You're laughing at me.' Lotty would have liked to have had the strength to pull away, but it felt too good with his big hand gentling down her spine and over the flare of her hip, and his fingers tightened on her.

'I am,' he agreed, the smile deepening. 'Why on earth would I mind?'

'I'm not your type,' said Lotty, but she eased closer anyway until her bare skin was pressed against his.

'Aren't you?' His palm was so warm, so sure against her that Lotty caught her breath.

'You said yourself that I'm not the kind of woman you're looking for,' she managed.

That was true. Corran was oddly jolted by the reminder. He shouldn't have needed reminding. His mother had been lesson enough and, after his ill-fated marriage to Ella, he had no intention of falling for another woman who wouldn't fit in with life here in Mhoraigh.

Corran was clear in his own mind. He wanted a practical, sensible woman who wanted to share his plans and work with him to restore the estate to its former glory. A woman who would belong at Mhoraigh and be part of his life for ever.

Lotty wasn't that woman. No matter how hard she worked, there was an elegance to her that made her look like an exotic orchid planted out in a kitchen garden.

And she wasn't going to stay. She had been clear about that.

But none of that had mattered last night when she had asked him to kiss her. All the reasons why it would be sensible to keep a distance had evaporated at one look from those beautiful grey eyes. He could have said that it wasn't a good idea, Corran realised in retrospect, but he could see how much it had cost Lotty to ask him and the truth was that he hadn't wanted to say no.

The truth was that kissing her was all he had been able to think about as they walked along the loch and the moment he had looked at her and seen the uncertainty and desire in her face he had been lost.

Last night had caught Corran unawares. He had

wanted to give Lotty pleasure, to make her first time special, but he hadn't expected to be shaken himself. She had been so sweet, though. So surprising. All his life he had kept a careful guard over his feelings, and it was unsettling to remember how easily it had been swept away by the feel of her skin, by the taste of her, by her warmth and aching innocence. By the heat that had blazed so unexpectedly between them and blotted out all sensible thought.

Sensible thought. He should be able to do that, at least. Corran hauled his mind back to more practical channels with difficulty. Lotty herself seemed to be approaching the matter pragmatically. Surely he could do the same?

'I was thinking about marriage when I said that,' he told her. 'I'm not ready to marry yet. And as you don't seem to be in any hurry to marry either, why shouldn't we make the most of the time we've got together in the meantime?'

Something flickered in the lovely grey eyes. Corran couldn't be sure if it was relief or disappointment. 'That's what I think,' she said. 'We both know that it's only temporary. I'll be leaving in a few weeks.'

CHAPTER SEVEN

LEAVING. A cold finger touched Corran's heart, but he pushed the feeling aside. 'That's settled, then,' he said, sliding a hand over her hip to draw her closer but she fended him off once more.

'It's just that the rest of the time, when we're not…you know…' She trailed off in confusion and Corran felt something shift in his chest at her blush.

'I know,' he said, doing his best to keep his smile under control, although he wasn't sure how well he succeeded as Lotty was looking at him suspiciously.

'Yes, well…the rest of the time, I want it to be the way it was before,' she said. 'I want to carry on working just the way I've been doing, and I want you to be just as crabby and cranky as you always are.'

'Cranky?' He had her warm against him once more, could kiss his way along the lovely slope of her shoulder. 'When am I ever cranky?'

'All the time,' said Lotty, but she sounded breathless.

'I'm not feeling very cranky at the moment,' he told her, smiling against her skin. 'You don't want me to be crabby now, do you?'

'Not now.' Lotty's hands were moving hungrily over his back, pulling him closer, pressing her nearer. 'Later then,' she managed unsteadily. 'Promise me you won't change.'

'I promise,' he said.

But it was difficult when the weather stayed fine for the most part, when the days drifted one into the other and the long summer evenings seemed more golden than usual. Corran found it harder and harder to be as cross as Lotty wanted. How could he be cranky when she was there, smiling at him? When, no matter how hard they had worked, there were long hours of sweetness to look forward to at the end of the day? He did his best to maintain the grouchy demeanour that seemed to mean so much to her, but even he could see it was less and less convincing.

Every morning, Corran told himself that he couldn't afford to lose focus on getting the cottages finished. Every morning he reminded himself that Lotty would be leaving.

There was no point in telling her his plans for the farm, Corran knew that, but still he found himself asking if she wanted to come with him to check on the sheep, found himself driving her up into the hills on the long summer evenings, walking with her across the heather. And if she stayed in the kitchen, as she often did, his step would quicken as he headed back to the house and, every time he caught sight of her, his heart lifted alarmingly.

Lotty was still persevering in her attempt to bake the perfect scone.

'I wish I'd never told you I liked scones,' he said, coming into the kitchen to find her sulking over another batch of leaden scones with burnt bottoms.

'I'm going back to Mrs McPherson,' grumbled Lotty. 'I'm sure she forgot some vital ingredient.'

Corran slid his hands around her waist and pulled her back against him so that he could kiss the side of her neck. He liked the way she arched when he kissed her there, liked the tiny breath she sucked in. He liked how he could make a smile tremble on her lips, no matter how cross she was.

Not that he was supposed to be noticing things like that. He was supposed to be thinking about the estate, not about how warm and sweet she was as she turned in his arms. Sure enough, she was smiling and the grey eyes were shining. He loved how transparent she was, how true.

Loved? Corran caught himself up on the word. No, that wasn't right. Liked, yes. Admired, yes. Loved, no.

No, no, no.

'What is it?' said Lotty, and he realised that he had let her go.

'Nothing.' She wanted him to be grouchy, he would be grouchy. Now he *felt* grouchy. 'I'd rather you spent time painting than making scones.'

'I've *been* painting,' she pointed out. She was on the third cottage and making good progress, as Corran well knew. 'I'm waiting for it to dry before I do the top coat in the bathroom. I should finish tomorrow.

'Which reminds me,' she said as she tipped the scones into the bin. 'Do you know what day it is tomorrow?'

'Thursday.'

She clicked her tongue. 'More important than that.'

'It's not your birthday, is it?'

'It's exactly a month today since we made that bet.' Lotty cocked her head on one side. 'You said I wouldn't last a day, and I bet you I'd still be here a month later. Remember?'

'Oh. That.' Corran shoved his hands in his pockets. 'Well, I've already admitted I was wrong.' He pretended to glower at her. 'What more do you want?'

'We had a deal,' Lotty reminded him. 'You promised to take me out to dinner.'

'All right.' Corran didn't mind doing that. She had earned a decent dinner. 'We'll go to Fort William on Saturday. There's a good restaurant on the loch there.'

But Lotty was shaking her head. 'I don't want to go to Fort William,' she said. 'I want to go to the ceilidh at the Mhoraigh Hotel tomorrow.'

She knew Corran wouldn't want to go. She could see him thinking of reasons not to.

'The food there is terrible,' he said after a moment.

'You don't care about food,' Lotty pointed out.

'I do if I'm paying for it.'

'We'll eat before we go. The point is the dancing, not the dinner.'

Corran rubbed a hand over his face. 'Wouldn't you rather go out for a nice meal?'

'No,' said Lotty. 'I want you to take me to the ceilidh.'

The past week had been a revelation. Nothing she had read in books had prepared her for how different she would feel. It was as if she had never been properly alive before, Lotty thought, as if she had been sleepwalking through life doing what was expected of her. Now every cell, every fibre of her was alight, on fire.

She loved making love with Corran. It was messier and more awkward and much, much more exciting than she had imagined, and it made her feel wild and reckless. She loved knowing that the rules changed the moment they closed the bedroom door and she didn't have to be sweet and good any more. She loved abandoning herself to the passion that flared between them every night, loved forgetting everything but the touch of Corran's hands, the feel of his lean, hard body, the taste of his mouth, the shivery, shocking excitement, the glittery rush.

But in the morning she remembered. In the morning the old Lotty was back, wagging a mental finger and pointing out that forgetting like that was a very bad idea. Reminding her that she would have to go home one day soon, and that there would be no more heart-shaking nights, no more bone-melting pleasure. There would be duty and responsibility and doing the right thing.

She would go back to Montluce and be the perfect princess once more, and Corran would be here alone. Lotty hated the thought of it. Self-sufficient he might be, but she wanted him to at least make contact with the village again. She'd wondered how to make it happen until she had driven to the shop in Mhoraigh that morning.

'Mrs McPherson was telling me about the ceilidh this morning,' she said to Corran. 'She says everyone goes. I think it sounds like fun.'

'It won't be if I go,' said Corran flatly. 'No one wants me there, and you know it.'

'Because they don't know you,' Lotty said. 'They've just got an image of you that you've never bothered to correct. I don't understand why you're not open with them. If you told them the truth and let them see you as you really are, they would change their minds. What's the point of pretending to be someone you're not?'

'I'm not pretending,' Corran said with a touch of irritation. 'They think I'm unfriendly and an outsider, and I am.'

'I've seen you up in the hills,' she reminded him. 'You belong here.'

'You won't get them to believe that.'

'If they saw what you're doing here, and knew what you felt about the estate, they would.'

'Frankly, Lotty, I don't care what they believe,' Corran said. 'They're not interested in me, and I'm not interested in them. I can't see how me going to the ceilidh is going to change that.'

'It's not all about you,' Lotty pointed out. 'I want to go.'

'Then go with Mrs McPherson. She seems to be your big buddy.'

Her mouth set in a stubborn line. 'I want to go with you.'

'The deal was for dinner,' Corran tried, scowling, but Lotty wasn't going to be intimidated out of her plan. Corran might not accept it, but he needed to be part of the village.

'Lucky you,' she said. 'I'm a cheap date.'

'I don't dance.' It was his last shot, and Lotty wasn't having any of it.

'Come on, Corran. You made the bet, and you lost.'

He tried to glare her down, but she just returned him stare for stare, and in the end he sighed irritably. 'Oh, very well. If that's what you want. But don't blame me if it's a disaster.'

'I thought you'd wear a kilt.' Lotty's face fell when she saw Corran waiting for her in black jeans and a dark shirt. He looked vaguely menacing, not helped by his forbidding expression.

'Lotty, you've got a ridiculously romantic notion of what this ceilidh is going to be like,' he said. 'No one will dress up for it. It's just a dance in a pub, not a formal ball.'

'Oh.' Lotty looked down at her acid yellow shift dress. 'Am I going to be overdressed?'

Corran studied her with mingled exasperation and affection. It wasn't that the dress was ostentatious. The style was spectacularly simple, in fact, but the cut and the material shrieked expense. She wore it with little pumps and her short hair was tucked behind her ears to show plain pearl earrings.

'Massively,' he said. 'You look like you're going to a cocktail party in Paris, not a ceilidh in a crummy country hotel.'

Lotty bit her lip. 'Do you think I should change?'

'No.' The trouble wasn't what she was wearing, it was the style with which she wore her clothes, the elegance with which she held her head. 'You're going to look out of place whatever you wear,' he told her. 'Let's just go and get this over with.'

The band was tuning up as they walked into the hotel's dining room, which had been cleared for the ceilidh. Silence fell at the sight of them, broken only by the scrape of the fiddle and the squeeze of the accordion. They could hardly have looked more alien, Corran thought. Himself, dark and forbidding, the unwanted son, and Lotty, bright and elegant and regal.

He had known it would be like this. There was no place for either of them in the village. Looking round the hostile faces, Corran wished that he had flatly refused to come. Not for himself, but he hated the thought that Lotty would be ostracised because she was with him. She would be hurt and upset, and the prospect was enough to make him reach for her arm, ready to swing her round and lead her back out before anyone could reject her.

But, not for the first time, Lotty surprised him. For someone with so little confidence in herself, she was undaunted by the hostile atmosphere. She moved forward, smiling, as if she had spent her life defusing awkward situations and, before Corran knew what was happening, she had put everyone at their ease and the party atmosphere resumed.

Watching her, Corran was puzzled and impressed. The surly Mhoraigh villagers unbent to a man in the face of her charm, and before long she was being swept off to dance by the burly Rab Donald, who had been Andrew's best friend when they were boys and who had eyed Corran himself with uncomplicated dislike.

The music struck up with a flourish, and the dance began with much swinging of partners and stamping of feet. The floor was full, but it was impossible to miss Lotty in her yellow dress, a bright light at the heart of the room. Next to Rab, she looked tiny, a delicate, elegant pixie.

Rab had his meaty hands at her waist. Corran's brows drew together.

'Now there's a fine girl.' Mrs McPherson spoke beside him, clearly following his gaze.

Fine. It was a good word to describe Lotty, Corran thought. There was nothing crude about her at all. From her delicate ears to her little feet, she was all pure lines and light.

He glanced at Mrs McPherson, then back to Lotty. 'Yes, she is. Except when it comes to cooking, of course.'

'How is she getting on with her scones?'

'They get worse and worse.'

Mrs McPherson laughed. 'She's always asking if I've left out some vital ingredient.'

Corran had always liked Betty McPherson, and she at least wasn't eyeing him askance the way the rest of them were. Lotty might have been accepted, but the others were still giving him a wide berth.

It was nice of Mrs McPherson to come and talk to him, but he was having trouble concentrating on the conversation when Rab was out there, touching Lotty, holding her. Corran could feel his hands curling into fists with the longing to push his way through the dance and punch Rab off her.

It surely had to be the longest dance in history, but at last the music ended. Corran's tense muscles relaxed. The dance was over. There was no need for Rab to touch her any more. And no need for Lotty to encourage him by smiling at him like that either.

But now she was laughing, agreeing to dance with Nick Andrews, who had owned the hotel as long as Corran could remember, and who made no secret of his dislike of Corran either. Corran's expression grew blacker but he managed to drag his attention back to Betty McPherson.

'I don't know why she's so obsessed with those bloody scones,' he said, and she smiled gently.

'She wants to make them perfect for you.'

There was a tiny silence, then Corran turned to her as the fiddle struck up once more for *Strip the Willow.* 'Would you care to dance, Mrs McPherson?'

'Betty,' she corrected him. 'And, thank you, I would.'

When it was Corran's turn to make his way down the line of ladies, he found himself face to face with Lotty at last. Holding out her hands so that he could swing her round, she smiled at him, such a joyous, shining smile that Corran felt something unlock in his chest. She looked so beautiful, he didn't want to let her go.

But, sooner or later, he was going to have to.

Lotty was obviously having a wonderful time, and her delight was infectious. She danced every dance, and Corran made himself stand back and let her meet everyone. He was uncomfortably conscious that he had been selfish. He had wanted to keep her to himself, but he could see now that Lotty needed more. She was happy now at Loch Mhoraigh, he knew that, but so perhaps had his mother been at the beginning. In the end she would want people, parties, more than just him.

Perhaps Lotty knew that herself. Perhaps that was why she was so insistent that she would be leaving. Perhaps it was just as well she was going.

Or so Corran tried to convince himself.

So he stood back and let the other men dance with Lotty, but when the leader of the band called everyone onto the floor for the last dance, he made sure that he was standing next to her. It would be a slower tune, he knew, and he pulled her onto the floor before anyone else had a chance to get his eager hands on her.

Now he could get his hands on her instead.

Corran held her, the way he had wanted to hold her all evening. He spread his fingers over her back, feeling the tiny bumps in her spine through the silk dress. Her hair was growing out of its pixie cut but if he ran his hand up to the nape of her neck, the skin there was still soft and enticing beneath the feathery wisps of hair. She was slender and warm in his arms, and he could smell the faint expensive fragrance she always wore in the evenings. He was going to miss that when she left.

He was going to miss a lot of things, Corran realised. Already he was used to her being in the kitchen, frowning down at the cafetière, wrinkling her nose at the smell of tea. He was used to the way she tied her hair up in a scarf like a Fifties housewife when she was doing dirty work. Only Lotty could carry *that* look off without looking ridiculous!

She had an innate style whatever she was wearing, he thought. In the evening she would change into a skirt or loose trousers after a bath, and Corran had to admit that her elegant, feminine presence had made a difference to the feel of the house. The rooms felt comfortable since Lotty had taken on the role of housekeeper. Corran wasn't quite sure how she had done it. They were still bare, but they felt lighter, happier, somehow. She found wild flowers in the overgrown garden and made charmingly haphazard arrangements with them. Even the kitchen looked mellow and inviting now, in a way it had never done before. Corran liked going in at the end of the day and finding her there.

He liked how eager and responsive she was in bed. How passionate. How she could make his senses reel with the brush of her lips.

Yes, he would miss her, Corran acknowledged to himself. But Lotty had made it very clear that she had no intention of staying for ever. She would be moving on soon.

And that was just as well, Corran reminded himself. Lotty wasn't the sort of wife he needed. She couldn't cook. She didn't understand the country.

She was ethereal and lovely, and he needed someone sturdy and strong. She was all wrong for him.

Still, he rested his cheek against her hair and felt
her relax wordlessly into him. He turned his lips
to her temple and touched the skin there. Her hand
tightened in his and she eased closer, her body soft
and pliant. The feel of her made him light-headed.
It made him forget that she was leaving, forget the
village and the hostility he still sensed beneath
the smiles, forget everything but the woman in
his arms. Lotty, who was all wrong, but who felt
so right.

'Please tell me it's not more scones!'

Lotty was at the range, peering dubiously into
the oven, but the moment Corran came into the
kitchen her pulse kicked up a notch. It always did
that, even now. It didn't matter where they were
or what they were doing, something inside leapt
at the sight of him every time.

'I thought I'd try a chocolate cake for a change,'
she told him as he dumped a couple of carrier
bags on the kitchen table. He'd had a meeting at
the bank in Fort William and grudgingly agreed

to stop off at the village shop on his way back to pick up a few essentials.

A man with shopping bags. Nothing glamorous or heroic about that, but he was so lean and so powerful, and his presence filled the room so that the breath dried in Lotty's mouth. It did that every time, too.

Lotty kept waiting to get used to making love with Corran. She had expected that it would slake that terrible craving to wind herself round him and press herself against him and crawl all over him, but if anything it was worse. She was still dazzled by lust and longing and the thrill of being able to touch him. After years of being a good girl, Corran's touch had let loose a different Lotty, one whose recklessness and passion both thrilled and alarmed her.

Only the day before she had finished painting the woodwork in the cottage's kitchen. It was too late to start a new room—or that was the excuse Lotty gave herself, anyway—so she went to find Corran. Perhaps she had it in mind to help him tidy up. Or perhaps she had something quite different in mind all along.

He was in the next cottage, boxing in the bath.

When Lotty paused in the doorway, he was bending over a sheet of plywood, sawing it into shape. The floor was covered in sawdust and wood shavings and the smell of new wood filled the air.

As Lotty watched, the sun came out from behind the clouds and a shaft through the open window lit directly onto Corran, hot and sweaty in a faded T shirt and jeans. She could see the dust hanging in the light. Her gaze followed the sunbeam to where it gilded the prickle of stubble on his jaw, to the curve of his back as he bent over the wood, to the muscles that flexed in his arms as he wielded the saw, and she was gripped by a need so acute that she couldn't move, couldn't even breathe. She could just stand and stare at him.

Sensing her gaze, Corran glanced up and froze at her expression. He didn't say anything but something shifted in the air, something hot and dark that lit the fever in Lotty's blood.

Corran laid down his saw and straightened.

She took a step inside the room.

'You're a bad girl,' he said, and his voice was dark and dusty with desire.

'I didn't say anything.'

'You didn't need to.'

He put his hands on the wall on either side of her, trapping her, and Lotty's heart pounded with excitement. She slid her hands beneath his T-shirt so that she could run them over his flanks, loving the feel of his warm, solid skin, revelling in the flex of his muscles beneath her touch, smiling at his indrawn hiss of breath.

'Do I need to say anything now?'

'No,' he said, and the expression in his eyes snarled every one of Lotty's senses into an urgent knot of desire.

And then…oh, then! Lotty still burned at the memory. It had been wild, exciting, reckless.

Very reckless.

'I'm going to have to be prepared if you're going to do that to me again,' Corran said unevenly at last, resting his forehead against hers.

'Do what?' Lotty was breathless. She clung to him, limp with satisfaction. 'What did I do?'

'You looked at me. You know what I mean,' he said as she started to laugh. 'You turned those great eyes on me and they told me you'd die if you couldn't have me.'

'That's how I felt,' she confessed.

'We mustn't do that again, Lotty,' said Corran. 'It's too much of a risk.'

'No,' she had agreed. It was stupid to make love without taking precautions, of course it was. But, deep down, Lotty loved the fact that she could be bad. That she could make him forget about everything but her, his hands on her, her mouth on his, make him forget about anything but the rocketing need between them.

That she could forget that she was a princess. Lotty loved that most of all.

Flushing with remembered heat, Lotty made herself turn back to the range and pull out the cake. How was it possible that it looked flatter and harder and thinner than it had when she'd put it in?

'I don't think it's supposed to look like this,' she said, her mouth turning down at the corners. It certainly didn't look like the exquisite patisserie that the palace kitchens produced. The head chef made a chocolate cake that was so light and delicious that it was hard to believe that it contained any calories at all. It melted in the mouth, so that one slice was never enough.

This cake had about as much chance of melting in the mouth as a brick.

'It'll be fine,' said Corran, without glancing at it. He was putting milk away in the fridge. 'Let's have some tea and we can always dunk the cake in it.'

'Good idea.'

Lotty put the kettle on. She had never cared for tea before, but now she drank it all the time. They often had a mug in the afternoon, taking a brief break from working.

The cottages were coming on really well. Lotty felt proud when she looked around her and remembered what a desperate state they had been in when she first arrived. She didn't mind getting dirty and tired. She could see the cottages being transformed in front of her eyes. She was *doing* something, not just having things done for her. Lotty sat on the doorstep with Corran and the dogs on those afternoons, and she watched the hills and drank tea and felt completely happy.

Every now and then the cold finger of reality would poke her in the stomach, reminding her that time was passing and this wasn't for ever, but Lotty's heart shrank back from dealing with it. One more week, she said to herself every time. One more week, and then she would face the prospect of leaving.

It was getting harder and harder to remember this wasn't her real life. Montluce felt very far away. Corran had offered her the use of his computer after she had told him she'd used the internet café in Fort William, so she had been able to check her email over the past month, but increasingly she found herself putting it off. She'd had a stiff message from Dowager Blanche, who was obviously hurt and angry, which made Lotty feel horribly guilty, as it was no doubt intended to, and she didn't want any more like that.

Caro's messages were much more entertaining. Lotty enjoyed seeing palace life through her friend's eyes. It made her realise how absurd all the formality she had taken for granted for years was. Lotty was glad Caro seemed to be having a good time, although she was suspiciously cagey about her relationship with Philippe. It sounded as if the people of Montluce had taken her to their hearts too.

Lotty even allowed herself a little fantasy that Caro would get together with Philippe. If the two of them married, Caro could be first lady of the realm and Lotty would be free. Then Lotty felt selfish. How could she wish the restrictions of royal life on her free-spirited friend? Besides, she couldn't see her grandmother accepting Caro as the future Crown Princess. The Dowager Blanche had firmly traditional views on who might or might not be acceptable to marry into Montluce's royal family. A commoner like Caro was unlikely to go down well.

Then there was Philippe to think about too. Lotty knew how difficult going back to Montluce even for a short time would be for him. He would be putting a good face on it, but his relationship with his father was too bitter for him to want to stay in the country a moment longer than necessary.

No, Caro and Philippe had done enough for her as it was. She couldn't expect them to take over her life on a permanent basis. She couldn't run away from her obligations for ever. She would have to go back to Montluce and do her duty, the way she had been raised to do.

But not yet, her heart cried. *Not yet.*

'Oh, I nearly forgot.' Corran drew a glossy magazine from the bottom of the carrier bag. 'Mrs McPherson sent you a present.'

'A present?' Surprised, Lotty set the two mugs of tea on the table and took the magazine. 'Really? For me?'

'She seemed to think you'd like it. I can't imagine why,' he said austerely as Lotty turned the magazine over to reveal the distinctive cover of *Glitz*. 'It's full of vacuous celebrities as far as I can see. Why would anyone care about all that trivial gossip?'

'It's called being interested in people,' said Lotty, who had been known to flick through a magazine in her time too.

She fanned the pages. 'Besides, it's not all gossip. There's also important stuff in here about shoes and frocks and make up. We're not all riveted by breeding programmes for Highland cattle, you know.'

'I forget you're interested in that kind of stuff,' said Corran, drinking his tea morosely.

'I wonder why Mrs McPherson thought I would be?' Lotty said, still puzzled.

He shrugged as she pulled out a chair and sat down. 'You seem to be her pet. I had to spend half the afternoon listening to her rabbiting on about scones and how wonderful everyone thinks you are now. Although she did say something about Montluce, now I come to think about it. She seems to know more about you than I do.'

Lotty looked at him sharply, unsure what to make of the faint undercurrent of…resentment? jealousy? bitterness?…she heard in his voice.

'Well, it was kind of her to think of me,' she said, careful to keep her expression neutral.

'Yes, except then I felt obliged to pay for it,' grunted Corran. 'It's probably a tried and tested sales technique of hers: make me feel guilty for not thinking of bringing you a present myself.'

'Oh, so it's a present from you, in fact?' said Lotty with a half smile.

'I don't think it counts as a present if you've been blackmailed into buying it!'

She laughed. 'Well, thank you, anyway,' she said, opening the magazine out on the table and licking a finger so that she could leaf idly through the pages one by one. 'A little frivolity makes a nice change.'

Corran was leaning against the kitchen counter, eyeing her morosely over the rim of his mug as she looked through the magazine, a tiny smile curling the corners of her mouth, long lashes downswept over the grey eyes. His gaze rested on the heart-shaking line of her cheek, and an ache for something he couldn't name lodged in his chest.

The truth was that Betty McPherson had made Corran feel bad. He hadn't thought of Lotty missing things like shopping and gossip, but of course she would. There was little scope for fashion at Loch Mhoraigh, but she still managed to look elegant and feminine. She was clearly someone used to a comfortable life, surrounded by fine things. Sooner or later, she would start to hanker for proper shops and things to do in the evening, he reminded himself. True, she hadn't complained about their absence yet, but she hadn't been there that long.

It just felt like forever. Corran struggled to remember what it had been like without her now, and when he tried to imagine the future when she was gone, he just came up with a terrifying blank.

He was going to have to try harder.

CHAPTER EIGHT

ELLA hadn't complained either at the beginning, he remembered. She had claimed at first that he was all she wanted but, once they were married, it turned out that she wanted a lot more than that. Corran wasn't enough at all. Every day, there had been something that he didn't do or didn't feel or didn't provide.

His mouth twisted, remembering that time. Ella had been constantly discontented, it seemed. She was disappointed that he spent so much time at work, resentful that he didn't surprise her with bunches of flowers or mini breaks in Paris or little pieces of jewellery and hurt that he didn't send her messages on the hour, every hour.

Corran had never understood why Ella needed proof that he loved her. He said it, and he'd meant it, and it seemed to him that ought to be enough, but Ella required constant reassurance that he had obviously failed to provide. She would plunge into despair, punishing him with floods of tears or sulky silences, and then go out and spend huge sums on her credit card which apparently made her feel better. Corran wondered if she was subjecting Jeff to the same treatment now, and hoped his old friend was dealing with it better than he had.

He couldn't imagine Lotty carrying on like that. She had a natural dignity and grace, a quiet strength apparent in the straightness of her spine and the tilt of her chin. But then there had been no warning that Ella was that needy either. He had married one woman and ended up with quite a different one, Corran remembered bitterly. He wouldn't make that mistake again.

And what, really, did he know about Lotty? He knew she was warm and passionate and stubborn. He knew she was hard-working and intelligent, but had an inexplicable lack of belief in her own beauty and abilities. He knew how her eyes lit when she smiled. He knew the scent of her skin, the softness of her hair, the precise curve of her hip. He knew she was stylish and sweet and a terrible cook.

But she was close-mouthed about her family and

life before she came to Loch Mhoraigh. If it ever came up in the conversation, she would change the subject, and Corran was happy to pretend that her other life didn't exist, that there was just this time they had together.

Her English was so perfect that he often forgot that she was from Montluce. Mrs McPherson's reminder had been like a finger poking in the ribs. He didn't like the idea that she had thought about Lotty being the kind of girl who would like to read a glossy magazine. He didn't like her knowing something about Lotty that he didn't. He didn't like being reminded that Lotty had another life in another country, where she probably shopped and read magazines and wore expensive clothes all the time.

Corran didn't want to know about that Lotty. That Lotty was going to leave. If he thought about that Lotty, he'd have to remember that she wasn't going to stay here at Loch Mhoraigh for ever. Watching her leaf through the magazine, remembering, Corran felt something cold settle in the pit of his stomach.

More fool him for forgetting in the first place. He had to get a grip, Corran told himself. He had lost focus on the estate. He was thinking about Lotty too much. He'd be knocking down a wall or plumbing in a new pipe, and he'd remember her softness, or the silkiness of her hair, or the way his heart pounded when she touched him, when he ought to be thinking about breeding programmes or investment strategies.

Lotty was sipping her tea, pursing her lips at a page, shaking her head at another as she flicked through the articles. They certainly didn't require much reading. From what Corran could see, they consisted of a lot of shiny photographs with captions. How could she possibly find any of it interesting?

Then she turned a page and choked, spluttering tea everywhere.

'What is it?' he asked.

But Lotty couldn't answer. She was coughing and laughing at the same time, her eyes watering, until Corran began to get concerned. Levering himself away from the counter, he patted her on the back.

'Are you OK?'

'I'm fine,' she tried to say, but it came out as a squeak and she put a hand to her throat. 'Sorry!'

Unthinkingly keeping his hand on her back,

Corran peered over her shoulder to see what had surprised her so much.

The page was dominated by a photograph of a vibrant girl with untidy hair. She was smiling at the camera and wearing a man's jacket that was clearly much too big for her. *A New Style Icon for Montluce,* trumpeted the headline.

Another picture showed her with a good-looking man. Corran read the caption. *Wedding Rumours for Prince Philippe,* it read.

'What's so funny?' he asked Lotty, who was still trying to clear her throat.

'What? Oh!' She tried to pull the magazine away. 'Oh, nothing. I was just surprised. She… she reminds me of someone I used to know, that's all.'

'Pretty girl,' Corran commented, studying the photo. He was still absently rubbing Lotty's back. 'At least she looks like she's got some personality, unlike most celebrities.'

Caro certainly had personality, thought Lotty. She was desperately aware of his warm hand moving over her, and she couldn't resist leaning back into it as she wiped her eyes.

She wished she could tell Corran about her

friend. She would have liked to have explained how Caro worried about her weight and wore the oddest clothes, like that old dinner jacket of her father's, and how much she would laugh to hear herself described as a style icon.

It would be nice to tell him what a special friend Caro was, and how she had stepped in to give Lotty herself a chance to escape from Montluce for a while. Caro would say that it had suited her too, but Lotty knew that it was a lot to ask her friend to give up two months of her life.

But how could she tell Corran all that without telling him that she was a princess? Without changing everything.

They had so little time left. Why risk spoiling it? They were going to have to say goodbye anyway, Lotty reasoned. She wanted Corran to remember her as a woman, not as a princess pretending to be someone she wasn't.

Unaware of her thoughts, Corran was still looking at the picture of Caro and Philippe. 'What an awful life, though,' he said. 'Who'd want it? I can't see the point of these tinpot monarchies, other than to fill the pages of trashy magazines.'

Tinpot monarchy? Lotty stiffened, unable to

let the insult pass. 'I'm from Montluce,' she reminded him in an icy voice. 'We don't think of it as a tinpot monarchy.'

'Oh, come on, Lotty! You're not telling me you believe the monarchy in a tiny place like Montluce isn't an anachronism?' Taking his hand from her shoulder, he flicked the picture of Philippe dismissively. 'What does this guy actually do other than get himself photographed? It's not as if any of them do any work.'

Lotty thought of the long days smiling and standing until her back ached, of putting people at their ease and making them feel as if they had been part of something special even if they had just shaken hands with her. At the end of the day her hand was sometimes so sore she had to soak it in iced water to reduce the swelling.

Abruptly, she pushed back her chair so that Corran had to move out of the way. She carried her mug over to the sink. 'I didn't realise you were such an expert on European monarchies,' she said coldly.

'I'm not, but I've got several mates who became bodyguards after leaving the Army. It's good money, I gather, but God, what a life, trailing around after obscure royals! Some of the stories they tell about the pampered brats they have to babysit would make your hair stand on end. They spend their entire day following these people around from shop to restaurant to party.'

'Really?' said Lotty, who had spent her entire life being shadowed by a member of the royal close protection team.

Montluce had few political problems, at least until the recent furore about the proposed gas pipeline, but it was an important financial centre, and the royal family's wealth was enough to make them a target. Lotty's first companions were lean, expressionless men whose eyes moved constantly and who were always on the alert to the slightest sound or movement.

'It's not much fun being trailed after either,' she pointed out, and then, as Corran raised his brows, 'I imagine.'

Rinsing out the mug, she set it upside down on the draining board and wiped her hands on a tea towel. 'I'd better get back to work,' she said.

Corran frowned. 'Haven't you finished for the day?'

'I've just a bit of tidying up to do.'

'The midges will be out soon,' he warned.

'I won't be long.'

Lotty needed to be alone for a while. It had been odd seeing Caro and Philippe in that magazine, and she hadn't been able to help laughing at the idea of Caro's unconventional dress style coming into fashion, but Corran's attitude to the Montlucian monarchy had stung. That was her family he had dismissed as being lazy, pointless and out of touch.

It was ironic that Philippe was probably the person who would most agree with him.

The conversation had depressed her, underlining as it did the gulf between them. It had left her feeling disloyal and guilty for being so happy at Loch Mhoraigh.

Calling for Pookie, she walked down to the cottages, her hands stuffed into her pockets. The little dog frolicked around her ankles and she thought about how much she would miss him when she left. The loch was grey and choppy under sullen clouds, and there was a rawness to the air that made Lotty zip up the collar of her fleece. On a day like this, it ought to be easy to feel nostalgic for the green hills and serene lakes of

Montluce but there was an elemental grandeur to the Scottish mountains that caught at Lotty's throat, no matter what the weather.

That made her feel bad too. She was a Princess Charlotte of Montluce. She loved her country. She shouldn't feel like this about another one, as if Scotland was where she belonged. As if it was going to tear her heart out when she left.

Lotty vented her confused feelings on the floor-boards, getting down on her knees to scrub them vigorously. She didn't want things to change, but they couldn't stay like this for ever.

She should start giving some thought to leaving soon. She had saved most of her housekeeper's wage, derisory though it was. She had enough to move on, and maybe get a job somewhere else for her last month of freedom.

Or perhaps she should just go home to Montluce. That was where she belonged, after all. Her grandmother might be autocratic, but Lotty was her only real family now and she would need her granddaughter's support.

Philippe would be leaving Montluce as soon as his father was well enough to take over his duties once more, and then Lotty would have to be ready to step back into the role she had been born for. But she couldn't go back to the way she had been before. Not after being here with Corran. Somehow she was going to have to do *something* to make her life bearable when she got home.

Then she caught herself up. Bearable? What kind of self-pitying nonsense was that? Lotty flinched inwardly, ashamed of herself. She had more money than she knew what to do with. Everyone loved her—the papers were always saying so. She never had to worry about where the next meal was coming from. Millions of people would love to be in her position.

They'd love to have nothing to do all day except be shown around factories and community projects. They'd love to shake hands and smile, no matter how fed up they were feeling. They'd love to have to be careful about everything they wore and everything they said and everything they did. They'd love to spend their lives living up to other people's expectations.

But she was the one going to have to do it.

And she would, Lotty vowed. As for the time she had left here with Corran, she would make the most of it and refuse to let herself have any regrets.

Corran had been right about the midges. Lotty had to run back to the house, frenziedly batting them away from her ears while Pookie scampered beside her, unclear about the reason for all the urgency but barking with excitement anyway.

In the kitchen, Corran had papers spread all over the table.

'Oh.' Lotty stopped, slapping the last few midges from her hands and neck. It was all very well to decide to make the most of things, but all at once the atmosphere seemed awkward. 'I was going to start the supper. Will I disturb you?'

'No, you carry on,' said Corran. 'I thought it would be easier to do this here than on the computer, but I can move if I'm going to be in your way.'

Why were they suddenly being so *polite* to each other? Lotty hated it. She washed her hands at the sink.

'What are you doing?'

'I heard back from the finance company I approached about investing in the estate this morning,' he told her. 'It just so happens that Dick

Rowland, one of the directors, is coming up to the Highlands with his wife. He suggested calling in on their way to Skye to have a look round the estate.'

'That's good news, isn't it?' It was difficult to tell from his expression.

Corran straightened the page of figures in front of him as if trying to decide. 'It goes against the grain to ask for help,' he said after a moment, 'but the fact is, I'm going to need extra money to get the estate up and running again, and I'm lucky to get any interest at all from investors in the current market. So yes, it's good news—but Rowland won't make up his mind until he's seen what we're doing.'

'I thought the idea was that income from the cottages would be ploughed back into the estate?' Lotty dug in the vegetable basket for an onion.

'It will be, but it's going to take a while for the money to start coming through. We might pick up one or two Christmas lets but, realistically, we won't get many takers until next Easter. I need to be investing in breeding stock this autumn. If Dick Rowland is prepared to invest in the estate, I can get going.'

Lotty picked up a knife and sliced the top off the onion. She was getting better at cooking basic meals, or perhaps she was just getting more practice. She was never going to be a master chef, but at least she didn't need to follow a recipe now to make shepherd's pie.

'So we need to impress him when he comes?'

Corran nodded. 'It won't be easy. Rowland's a famously hard-headed businessman. He says it'll just be an informal visit, but when I mentioned it to the bank manager today, she said I should have all my figures ready for him anyway.

'That's what I wanted to talk to you about before we got distracted by *Glitz,*' he went on stiltedly after a moment's hesitation. 'Are you likely to be around?'

'Around?' The onion was making Lotty's eyes stream, and she lifted her arm to wipe the tears away with the back of her wrist. 'What do you mean?'

'The Rowlands aren't coming for another month,' he said. 'You always said you'd only stay a couple of months.' Corran drew a breath. 'I wondered if you had a plan to move on yet.'

'Oh…' Lotty lowered the knife. Hadn't she just

decided that she should think about leaving? But she couldn't go, not while he needed her. 'No... not yet,' she said slowly.

'I'd appreciate it if you could stay a couple of weeks longer until they've been,' he said formally. 'I'd like to make sure the cottages are completely ready. It will show that I've got a strategy and can implement it.'

Lotty felt as if she'd been given a reprieve. Another month, and a reason to stay. Happiness was ballooning inside her, but the sober, sensible part of her brain hung in there too, dragging her back to reality with the reminder that nothing had changed really. She would still have to go.

'I'm happy to stay until they've been,' she told him, 'but after that...'

'You'll leave,' Corran finished for her quickly. 'I understand.'

Lotty didn't want him to understand. She wanted him to seize her in his arms and beg her not to go. She wanted him to refuse to let her go, to make her stay for ever.

But what about her grandmother? Her duty? What about the fact that Corran wanted a sensible, practical wife to share his life?

She forced a smile and went back to chopping her onion. 'So what's the plan? Finishing the cottages?'

'Yes, those first,' he said, pushing the papers into a pile. 'Then I'd like to get the rest of the place spruced up a bit too. Half the fences are down. It all looks shabby. I need to do something about the barns and pens, and the stable block is a mess… Well, I can't tackle all of it yet, but if I can cost out my development plans and look as if I've put in a bit of effort, I should have a better chance of convincing him that this can be a profitable estate again—and that's all he'll be interested in.'

Lotty wasn't sure about that. 'I think you should do something about the house too,' she said as she tipped the onion into a frying pan.

Corran frowned. 'The house is bottom of my priority list.'

'First impressions count,' she said.

She should know. She thought about all the royal visits she had done, and how everything was always tidy, always freshly painted and sparkling clean. It was nonsense to think that she was seeing places as they really were. The people who welcomed her wanted her to see them as they could be, as they longed to be, not as they were on a day-to-day level.

Corran wasn't convinced. 'The house isn't part of the investment plan.'

'They're going to arrive here,' Lotty pointed out. 'I'm not suggesting you do up the whole house, but at the very least you need to make sure the drawing room and the loo look welcoming.'

'I can't believe Dick Rowland will notice that the drawing room is a bit shabby.'

'His wife will. And it's more than *a bit shabby*. You don't want them feeling depressed by the place before they even get outside.'

Corran thought about that. 'I can't afford new furniture.'

'We can use some of the stuff we bought for the cottages,' said Lotty. 'As long as we've fully furnished a couple of those, they'll get the idea. We just need a couple of sofas and a coffee table. We'll keep it simple.'

She shook the onion in the pan, excited by the possibilities. 'It wouldn't take long to strip off the old wallpaper so you can't see the marks where the paintings were—that would make a big difference!—and we could sand the floorboards. I can make it look nice.

'If you want to impress this guy, Corran, you need to make sure you welcome him properly,' she said. 'I know what I'm talking about,' she promised him.

'I suppose you did this kind of thing in your PR job,' said Corran, and she bit her lip. She'd forgotten about her imaginary career in public relations.

'Something like that,' she said.

A thought occurred to her. 'How long are they going to stay?' she asked Corran, not sorry to change the subject. 'Not the night?'

The pale eyes gleamed with understanding. 'No, he said they were planning to spend the night in Fort William.'

'Phew! At least I won't need to produce a fancy meal.'

'I'll suggest a cup of tea,' said Corran. 'Just buy a packet of shortbread or something.'

But Lotty had no intention of giving the Rowlands shop-bought anything. She might not be up to cooking a gourmet meal, but surely she could manage something for tea. What better occasion could there be for some perfect little scones? And they *would* be perfect this time. She would go back to Betty McPherson and learn how to make them properly if it was the last thing she did.

It would be the last thing she did for Corran, and Lotty was determined to do it right. While she was doing her royal duty, she wanted to think of him here, on a thriving estate, doing what *he* needed to do. And if this investment helped him to achieve that, she would do whatever she could to make it happen.

Lotty was really pleased with the cottages when they were finished. Corran had put in new kitchens and bathrooms and done the tiling, while she had cleaned and painted them all. Now new carpets had been laid, and the rooms were simply but stylishly furnished. With that spectacular setting too, how could the Rowlands not be impressed?

Corran wanted to concentrate on the outside after that, but Lotty set about pulling the tired wallpaper off the drawing room walls. The house had much bigger rooms than the cottages, of course, and the high ceiling proved a new challenge. She had to balance precariously on ladders to reach the wallpaper underneath the coving, until Corran came in and shouted at her for taking unnecessary risks.

'It is necessary,' Lotty protested from the top of her ladder and he clicked his tongue in exasperation.

'*I'll* do it, then. Get down from there at once! I haven't got time to deal with you if you break your neck,' he grumbled.

It was almost like it had been before.

Almost.

Lotty couldn't quite put her finger on what had changed, but *something* had. There was an edge of desperation to their love-making now and, although they still talked and Corran was still grouchy, sometimes a constraint crept into the silences between them. Now those pauses in the conversation which had once been companionable seemed to be weighted with all the things they weren't talking about, like what would happen after the Rowlands had been.

Like the future, when they would go their separate ways.

Like saying goodbye.

Lotty was making more of an effort to keep in touch with Montluce, hoping that she would start to feel homesick. She wanted to remember all the things she loved about her country: the history and the proud independence of the people, the gentle lakes and the wooded hills, the cuisine and the markets and the chic way the women wore the most ordinary of clothes.

She emailed Caro more regularly, and was one of the first to hear when Philippe defied his father and the Dowager Blanche to refuse permission for the proposed gas pipeline that had caused unprecedented protests in the country. The environmental impact was too great, Philippe had decided, and astounded observers by negotiating a new agreement that miraculously satisfied the activists and those who were more concerned by the impact on the economy.

'Montluce has hit the headlines,' said Corran, who'd read about it on the internet. 'Your Prince Philippe is being hailed as a hero of the environment.'

'See, there's a point to him after all,' said Lotty, but she was wondering what was really happening in Montluce.

She hadn't heard from Caro for a while. The Dowager Blanche would be furious. Lotty's father hadn't taken much interest in anything beyond Ancient Greece, so it was her grandmother who had been running the country behind the scenes for years. She was the one who had made the original agreement for the pipeline, and she wouldn't take kindly to her will being crossed.

Expecting a crisis, Lotty was a little puzzled when none seemed to materialise but she had other things to think about. In spite of all her efforts to reconnect with Montluce, she was absorbed in life at Loch Mhoraigh. Sanding floorboards, walking the dogs, washing dishes, poring over a recipe, sweeping and tidying… Lotty clung to the ordinary things while she could, committing the simple joy of day-to-day life to her memory.

And when the day's tasks were done, there were the long, sweet nights with Corran. She hoarded every moment. Each touch, each kiss, each gasp of wicked pleasure was dipped in gold and stored in her head for the future when memories would be all she would have.

How could she think about Montluce when there was Corran, his sleek, powerful body, his mouth—his *mouth*—and those strong, sure hands? Lotty wanted to burrow into him, to hold on to him as if he could stop the hours passing and make it always *now,* and never *then.*

But the clock kept ticking on and, just when Lotty had let herself forget about life in Montluce, she received an email message from her grandmother that jolted her back to reality.

Caro, it seemed, had gone back to England and everything had gone wrong. Where was Lotty when she was needed? Her grandmother missed her. Please would she come home soon.

It was a querulous message, so unlike the indomitable Dowager Blanche that Lotty was instantly worried. Her grandmother never begged, never admitted that she needed help.

Lotty bit her lip.

Unseeingly, she looked out of the office window. It was a dismal evening with rain splattering against the glass and an angry wind rattling the panes, but Lotty was thinking about the palace in Montluce. Did her grandmother need her now? Had she been selfish long enough?

'May I use the phone?' she asked Corran, who was in the kitchen, poring over figures for his breeding programme.

He looked up, and his brows drew together at her expression.

'Of course,' he said.

Lotty went back to the office, took a deep breath, picked up the phone and dialled the palace's number. As soon as it was answered she gave the code word which put her call immediately through to the Dowager Blanche's office, and then there was a click and her grandmother herself on the line.

'Grandmère?' Lotty's throat tightened unaccountably at the sound of her grandmother's voice.

'Charlotte!'

The Dowager Blanche, realising that her granddaughter was on the line, proceeded to give Lotty a lecture on how selfish and irrational she had been.

Lotty bore it, insensibly reassured to hear that her grandmother was still on her usual intransigent form. From what she could tell, the Dowager was unsure who to be more cross with, Caro, Philippe or Lotty herself. It seemed that they were all ungrateful and irresponsible. Caro had gone back to England—not that the Dowager cared!— and Philippe was moping around. She was beaten and tired, her grandmother told Lotty, but she didn't sound it. She sounded like an old lady whose will had been thwarted and who didn't understand what was going on.

'When are you going to stop this nonsense and come home?' she demanded at last.

'Soon, Grandmère, I promise. There's just something I need to do here.'

'What sort of something? And where is *here?* What kind of granddaughter won't even tell her grandmother where she is?'

The querulous note in her voice stabbed at Lotty's conscience, but she steeled herself. 'I'll tell you about it when I come home.'

She ended the call and sat for a while, holding the phone against her chest, before she set it back in its cradle and went to find Corran.

'Problem?' he asked, looking up from his papers.

Lotty hugged her arms together. 'No...I'm not sure,' she confessed. 'Things seem to have gone wrong. My grandmother sounds OK, but I think she needs me.'

'Do you want to go home?' Corran made himself ask.

She hesitated, then shook her head. 'Not yet. I

don't think there's much I can do for now. I'll stay until after the Rowlands have been.'

'And then?'

Lotty drew an uneven breath. 'Then I'll have to go.'

'This looks…incredible.' Corran stared around the drawing room, amazed at the transformation.

Having banished Lotty from ladders, he had painted the ceiling and coving, and helped her carry in the furniture, but everything else she had done herself. The dusty floorboards had been sanded until they were a warm honey colour, and she had painted the walls a pale yellow so that the room seemed to be filled with sunshine even on the dullest of days.

Lotty had chosen two of the simple sofas they had bought for the cottages, and set them on either side of the fireplace with a sturdy coffee table between them. The only decoration was an arrangement of wildflowers in the grate. Bare the room might be still, but it looked stylish and welcoming too.

'Incredible,' said Corran again, remembering how sad the room had looked before.

'Let's hope the Rowlands think so,' said Lotty. 'Now all we need is a nice day so they can see Loch Mhoraigh at its best.'

That last morning, Lotty woke early. She lay for a while blinking at the morning sun that striped the bed and glinted off the hairs on Corran's chest. He was still asleep. Her face was pressed against his warm shoulder, and she could hear him breathing slow and steady.

Lotty's hand drifted down his arm. She didn't want to wake him, but she had to touch him. His muscles were firm beneath her palm, and her fingers played with the flat hairs on his forearm before curling around his wrist. How many more minutes would she be able to lie like this, drinking in the scent of his skin, comforted by his size and solidity and strength, loving him?

Of course she loved him. Lotty hadn't wasted time trying to deny it to herself. She even thought Corran might love her too, but not enough to give up Loch Mhoraigh. She knew what this place meant to him. She wouldn't ask him to leave it to live in Montluce with her, even if she had the courage to tell him who she was. Corran would

hate the formality of the palace, and her grandmother would be horrified.

And how could she turn her back on her grandmother and her country to stay here when Corran
had made it so clear that he was looking for quite
a different kind of woman to share his life?

No, they had agreed to a temporary affair, and it
had been wonderful, more wonderful than Lotty
could ever have imagined, but it would be better
for both of them if they left it at that.

If only Dick Rowland was impressed enough to
invest in the estate. Lotty told herself that it would
be easier to leave if she knew that Corran would
have the money to bring Loch Mhoraigh back to
life. He would be happy here.

And she would be happy in Montluce. Somehow.

CHAPTER NINE

LOTTY'S stomach churned and she shifted uneasily. She had been feeling queasy a lot recently. She'd tried to convince herself that it was anxiety about the Rowlands' visit but, deep down, she knew that it was dread at the prospect of saying goodbye. Once today was over, she would have no excuse to stay. She had promised her grandmother that she would go home, and that was what she would do, but oh, it was going to be hard!

'You're fretting,' Corran said lazily without opening his eyes.

'I thought you were asleep.'

'How can I sleep with you twanging beside me?' he grumbled, but he pulled her hard against him. 'Stop worrying,' he said as his hands slid possessively over her. 'It'll be fine.'

Lotty wasn't sure about that, but she let herself be distracted. She let him banish apprehension with skilful hands, let pleasure blot out all thought, and afterwards she pretended that nervousness about the day was all it had been.

She spent the morning fussing around, and made Corran change into a better shirt, although he refused point blank to put on a tie.

'I'm supposed to be a working farmer,' he said. 'Farmers don't wear ties.'

Lotty agonized for a while about her own outfit. She was afraid that some of her Montlucian clothes would look too elegant. As Corran pointed out, if she could afford clothes like that, it would look as if they didn't need investment, but she could hardly wear her old working clothes either. In the end she settled for her faithful jeans and the raspberry pink cardigan she had worn every evening when she first arrived.

'What do you think?' she asked Corran. She offered a nervous twirl. 'Is this casual enough?'

Corran looked her up and down, and his pale eyes were warmer than Lotty had ever seen them before. 'You look perfect,' he said.

Lotty was still glowing with his approval when the Rowlands arrived.

With its encouraging tax regime, Montluce had an impeccable reputation as a centre of in-

ternational finance and Lotty had met plenty
of financiers over the years. She had expected
Dick Rowland to fit the same suave mould, but
he turned out to be a bulky Yorkshireman with a
meaty face and small, sharp eyes. His wife, Kath,
was blonde and bubbly. She started talking before
she was even out of the car and barely drew breath
after that.

At least she seemed to like what she saw. 'Oh,
this is gorgeous!' she exclaimed, looking around
her. 'What a wonderful place to live.'

Her wide blue eyes came back to rest on Lotty's
face with a slight frown. 'Sorry, am I staring?' she
said when Corran introduced Lotty as his partner.
'You look so familiar… We haven't met before,
have we?'

Lotty's heart took a nosedive. Please, God, don't
let them have visited Montluce, she prayed. Why
hadn't she thought of that as a possibility? She had
hosted countless receptions for visiting bankers
at the palace. What if the Rowlands had been to
one?

She fixed a smile on her face. 'I don't think so,'
she said. 'I'm sure I would remember if we had.'

'Maybe you look like an actress,' said Kath, still puzzling. 'Who does she look like, Dick?'

To Lotty's relief, Dick ignored his wife. He was talking to Corran about the state of the track. 'You need to do something about that,' he said. 'I thought I was going to lose my sump at the very least on the way here.'

'I've included the cost of upgrading the track in the financial plan,' Corran told him.

Lotty offered coffee, but they agreed to begin with a tour of the estate. Corran drove them all in the Land Rover, which had been specially cleaned for the occasion. After admiring the cottages, he took them on a bumpy ride up the hillside to where he could point out the features of the estate and tell Dick about his plans for improvement.

It was a bright, breezy day. Billowing clouds bustled past the sun and sent great patches of light and shade sweeping across the hills. Far below them, the loch shone silver and Lotty remembered her first sight of it. Now it all felt so familiar.

It felt like home.

Lotty wanted to stand and drink in the view while Corran and Dick talked business but Kath Rowland kept chatting in her ear. She was determined to remember who Lotty reminded her of, and worked her way through a number of actresses, none of whom she remotely resembled, before deciding that it must after all be one of the mothers at her daughter's school. To Lotty's dismay, Kath appeared to be almost as avid a reader of gossip magazines as Betty McPherson. Why couldn't she be languid and sophisticated like most of the financiers' wives she'd met?

It was a relief when they went back to the house and she could escape to the kitchen to make tea. She had made the scone mix earlier so she just added milk and put them in the range while she boiled the kettle and set the tray. Wondering how Corran was getting on in the drawing room, she nearly forgot about the scones and had to whisk them out of the oven.

They were perfect.

She broke one open just to check. It was golden on the outside, light as air in the middle. Lotty could hardly believe it.

She carried the tray through to the drawing room, and her eyes met Corran's as she set it down on the low table between the sofas. She saw him register the immaculate scones and they exchanged a private smile.

'I've got it!' Kath's exclamation made Lotty jump. 'I've been racking my brain to remember who you remind me of, and it's just hit me. You're the spitting image of Princess Charlotte of Montluce!'

Lotty went cold and then hot. 'Oh, do you think so?' she said as casually as she could. 'Doesn't she have dark hair?'

'That's true,' said Kath, frowning in an effort of memory. 'She has that wonderful signature bob. Still, the resemblance is remarkable. You even have the same name. Lotty's short for Charlotte, isn't it?'

'Yes, it's quite a coincidence.' Lotty's hand shook slightly as she poured the tea. She could feel Corran's eyes on her face but she didn't dare look at him.

Kath was still talking. 'I feel so sorry for that poor girl,' she confided. 'They say that family is cursed. First her father died, then her uncle and his son, and wasn't there another son who was disinherited? He's in prison for murder.'

It was for a drugs offence, but Lotty wasn't

about to correct her. Smiling brightly, she picked up the plate and passed it to Kath. 'Would you like a scone?'

'Ooh, these look gorgeous!' Kath took one, but Lotty's hopes that she might be diverted were soon dashed. Kath had more to say about Princess Charlotte.

'Then she was engaged to Prince Philippe and he dumped her for somebody nobody had ever heard of. Poor thing, it must have been so humiliating for her!'

Desperately, Lotty offered scones to Dick and Corran, head ducked as if she could make herself invisible somehow.

'They say Charlotte is broken-hearted,' Kath went on inexorably. 'She just dropped out of sight.'

'Really?' said Corran. His voice was empty of all expression, but when Lotty risked a fleeting glance at him she saw that he was watching her steadily and unsmilingly.

He knew. She could see it in his eyes, which were the clear, cold blue of icebergs. Lotty thought about the warmth she had seen there before the Rowlands arrived and she wanted to weep. *You look perfect,* he had said.

'Nobody's seen her for ages,' Kath was rambling on. 'Well, she couldn't hang around and watch her fiancé flaunting another woman, could she? I don't blame her for lying low.'

She had to say something. 'I don't think they were actually engaged, were they?' she managed through stiff lips.

'Oh, yes, they were,' said Kath with all the authority of a regular *Glitz* reader. 'She absolutely adored Philippe. It's not surprising. He's absolutely gorgeous, although they say he's a real playboy.'

They didn't know anything, Lotty wanted to shout at her, but she had to sit there and listen to Kath speculating about Philippe and Caro, and pitying poor Princess Charlotte who was so beautiful and good and so astronomically wealthy but so unlucky in love.

'It just goes to show nobody can have everything, doesn't it?' she said.

It was a nightmare. Kath went on and on about Montluce and Lotty couldn't think of a single way to stop her. Her perfect scones tasted like ashes in her mouth.

After that one glance, she couldn't bear to look

at Corran again. He wasn't saying anything, but she could feel the cold fury radiating from him as clearly as if he had touched her. They were sitting rigidly side by side on the sofa facing the Rowlands, and the air between them was jangling with such tension that Lotty couldn't believe that Kath hadn't noticed.

'She's probably getting legless on some yacht somewhere,' Dick Rowland interrupted his wife at last. 'Corran, have you thought about a fish farm?'

So then they had to have a long discussion about the merits of salmon versus trout. Lotty crumbled her perfect scone on her plate and couldn't decide whether she longed for them to go, or dreaded it because then she would have to face Corran.

It felt as if she sat there for hours before Dick finally slapped his hands on his thighs and announced that they would have to get on the road. He hauled himself to his feet, followed reluctantly by his wife.

'I think you've got something here,' he said to Corran. 'Send me those figures, and we'll talk when I get back from Skye.'

Outside, he thanked Lotty for the tea. 'Those

were the best scones I've ever tasted,' he told her and then turned to shake hands with Corran. 'You're a lucky man, Corran, to have found yourself such a good cook!'

Dick was clearly waiting for Corran to put his arm around Lotty and smile and agree that he was a lucky man, but Corran couldn't bring himself to touch her. To touch the missing Princess of Montluce. Because of course that was who she was. He'd seen her expression. Only a fool wouldn't have guessed the truth long ago.

A fool like him.

Somehow Corran summoned a brief smile and managed to unlock his jaw enough to thank Dick for coming.

Face set, he stood next to Lotty—no, next to *Princess Charlotte*—on the doorstep and waved the Rowlands off. In silence they waited until the car had negotiated the bend in the track.

'Well, I think that went well, don't you, *Your Highness*?' he said at last.

Lotty flinched at the unpleasant emphasis on the title, but she didn't deny it. 'I think it did, yes,' she said and turned to go back inside.

Her coolness enraged Corran so much that he

grabbed at her arm before he remembered just who she was and snatched his hand back as if he'd been stung. 'You've been lying to me!'

'How?' Her face was pale, but her chin was up. How could he ever have mistaken her for anything but a princess? 'How have I lied, Corran?' she demanded. 'I told you that I lost my purse. That wasn't a lie. I told you I needed a job. That wasn't a lie. I told you that I wanted to get away for a while but that I couldn't stay for ever. That wasn't a lie either. I haven't lied about anything important.'

'What about omitting the tiny little bit of information about you being a princess?' he said furiously.

'Would it have made a difference?'

Corran was thrown by her cool challenge. 'A difference to what?'

'To whether you'd let me stay. To whether you'd have made love to me. To everything.'

He rubbed a distracted hand over his face. 'Yes! No! I don't know!'

Lotty smiled sadly. 'That's why I didn't tell you,' she said.

Without another word, she turned and went back

into the drawing room, where she began to gather up the teacups as if nothing had happened, as if his world hadn't just been turned upside down.

'You must have thought I was an idiot!' Corran followed her, too angry and humiliated to let it go. 'I can't believe I didn't see it before. There was so much that didn't add up. I should have guessed what you were. Who else but a princess wouldn't know how to make a cup of tea? Why didn't you tell me?'

'I couldn't!' Lotty's voice rose, and she let the cups and saucers clatter onto the tray. 'I didn't want to tell you! I didn't *want* you to start treating me carefully, the way everyone else does. Just once, just for a short while, I wanted someone to look at me and see *me,* not a princess.' She pressed a fist to her chest. *'Me!'*

There was a silence. Corran's gut churned with disappointment and dismay as he stared at her, trying to see the old Lotty in the princess with the flashing eyes and the hectic flush along her cheekbones.

'So what exactly are you doing here?'

'I'm being selfish.'

Without warning, the fury drained out of her

and she dropped onto the sofa as if someone had knocked her legs out from beneath her.

'Everything I told you about my family was true,' she said, looking down at her hands. 'Except I didn't tell you that Papa was Crown Prince of Montluce. He was a gentle man, and I don't think he ever got over my mother dying when she did. He retreated into his studies, and my grandmother ran the country behind the scenes far more effectively than he could ever have done.'

Lotty risked a glance at Corran, who had folded his arms and was listening with a grim expression. How was she going to make him understand what her life in Montluce was like?

'Papa was more interested in Ancient Greece than in shaking hands,' she went on after a moment. 'That was my job. As soon as I left school, I stepped into my mother's shoes and became the public face of Montluce. I didn't have a choice,' she tried to explain, hating the desperation that curled the edges of her voice. 'I'm an only child. Papa was wrapped up in his own world, my grandmother is elderly. I couldn't refuse. I was brought up to do my duty and I did it.

'Montluce may be a tinpot country to you,

Corran, but it matters to the people who live there. Wherever I go, people are delighted to see me. I'm loved by thousands. They all think I'm wonderful. They all think I'm beautiful. I'm their perfect princess,' said Lotty dully. 'I can't disappoint them by behaving badly, so I don't. I let them put me up on a pedestal, and then I realised I couldn't get down.'

'So how did you get from the pedestal to Loch Mhoraigh?' Corran's voice was as hard as his expression.

Lotty let out a long sigh. How could someone like Corran possibly understand?

'Worse than realising that I was stuck was realising that I didn't know what I was doing up there in the first place,' she said. 'Why do all those people love me? It has to be because of *what* I am—how could it be because of *who* I am? Nobody knows who I am, least of all me.'

She paused. Corran was listening, but it was impossible to tell what he was thinking. 'My family has a proud history. It's full of individuals who fought for Montluce and what they believed was right. I'm not like them. I've never had to fight for anything. I've never been tested.'

'That's not true,' said Corran angrily. 'For God's sake, Lotty, you coped with losing your mother at twelve and being sent away to school. How much more tested do you want to be?'

'I just didn't feel as if I had ever had a chance to discover who I really was,' she said. 'When Papa died, I was sad, but I thought that at last I'd have the chance to step out of the limelight and find a life of my own. The new Crown Prince had a wife, so they didn't need me. But then my uncle died, and his son soon afterwards, and it seemed like every time I turned round there was another family tragedy.'

Lotty smiled sadly. 'Someone had to represent the family while everything was in turmoil, and how could I refuse when everyone was depending on me? Now we've got Crown Prince Honoré. He doesn't have a wife either, and his only heir is his son Philippe. My grandmother decided it would be a good thing if Philippe and I made a match of it, and I…I panicked. I felt as if I was suffocating. I've never been good at standing up to my grandmother, and I could see all my opportunities closing down, one after the other.'

Leaning forward, she straightened the saucers

on the tray. 'I knew I couldn't run away for ever, but I was desperate to get away, just for a while. I wanted to do something for myself, to find out what life was like off the pedestal, so I made a plan with Philippe.'

'The same Philippe who broke your heart?' asked Corran with a scowl.

'It wasn't like that,' said Lotty. 'Kath had it all wrong.'

'What *was* it like?'

So she told him about the deal she had made with Philippe and Caro, and how they had provided the excuse for her to escape for a while.

'But now it's all gone wrong,' she said. 'I don't know what happened. Caro's gone home and my grandmother is upset and Philippe sounds desperate. And I have to go home,' she said dully.

'Back to the pedestal?'

'Back to my duty.' Lotty lifted her eyes to his once more. 'I'm a princess. I can't do whatever I like. I have a position, and with that comes responsibilities.' She swallowed. 'I ran away from them for a while, but they're still there.'

'So these last few weeks have just been a game to you while you played at being ordinary?'

In a dim part of his mind, Corran knew that he was being unfair, but discovering that Lotty was a princess had left him feeling raw and foolish. And hurt that she hadn't trusted him enough to tell him the truth. He'd always thought of her as transparent and true. Now he was wondering just how much of what she'd told him, how much of what she'd *been,* had been pretence.

Lotty bit her lip. 'I wanted to know what life is like without everyone watching your every movement, listening to your every word in case you make a mistake. Was that so bad?'

'You should have told me,' Corran said stonily.

Wearily, Lotty got up and put the last plates on the tray. 'What would have been the point?' she asked. 'There was never any question that we would have a future together. I didn't want to complicate things.'

'So that's it?'

'What else is there to say?' Lotty's voice was very calm, but her knuckles were white as she gripped the tray and carried it through to the kitchen. 'We both knew this was a temporary affair, Corran. I told you that I would have to go home to my grandmother, and I think I'd better do that now.'

'How are you going to do that?' he demanded furiously.

'I just need to lift the phone, and someone will come and get me.' Lotty turned on the hot tap and held her hand underneath it to check the temperature, while Corran stared at her incredulously.

'What the hell are you doing?'

'Washing up.' She glanced at his face. 'You see, I knew it would be like this. You think princesses shouldn't wash up.'

'I don't know *what* I think any more,' Corran confessed.

He dropped into a chair at the kitchen table and dragged his hands through his hair as if he could pull his thoughts into some kind of order.

Too late, he realised that he had fallen in love, but he loved *Lotty,* not this cool, distant princess. He loved Lotty, who was sweet and true, or who he thought was sweet and true. How could he know any more?

And even if she was still the same Lotty, how could he tell her that he loved her now? A declaration of love following straight on from the discovery that she was a princess and—what was that phrase Kath Rowland had used?—*astronomically wealthy,* was hardly likely to be convincing.

The truth crouched like a boulder low in his belly. Why hadn't he heeded his own instincts, which had warned him from the first that Lotty was trouble? Instead he had blundered on, forgetting Ella, forgetting the facts, forgetting everything but the smooth warmth of Lotty's skin, and the sweetness of her mouth, and the insistent pulse of need. And look where it had got him, a fool sitting at his own kitchen table while everything he had thought was true evaporated into nothing.

Lotty finished washing up and dried her hands on a tea towel. She glanced at Corran and hesitated, but in the end all she said was, 'I'll go and ring the palace now.'

Corran was still sitting at the table, his chest burning, his throat tight with bitterness and anger, when she came back.

'They're coming to pick me up.'

'Now?'

She looked out of the window to where the hills glowed in the early evening sun. 'There's plenty of light,' she said.

Sure enough, the faint purple sky was only just starting to deepen when Corran heard the dull wop-wop-wop of a helicopter overhead. He stood at the front door and watched it touch down perfectly on the gravel he had cleared for Dick Rowland, sending the birds shrieking in outrage from the trees.

Corran had seen plenty of helicopters in his time, but this one looked alien, sleek and shiny against the backdrop of the hills. It looked wrong.

The dogs were barking furiously at it. Corran called Meg back with a sharp word, but Lotty had to bend quickly to pick up Pookie, who, undaunted by his small size, was bristling with eagerness to see off the intruders.

Before the helicopter was settled, officers in dark uniforms had jumped out and were ducking under the still-spinning blades. They came quickly towards the house, guns at the ready, their eyes moving rapidly between him and Lotty. Corran kept his hands in full view. He'd been on operations like this himself, and these officers were professionals. They weren't taking anything for granted.

The lead officer spoke briefly to Lotty in French,

and she replied in the same language. Presumably she told them that she was under no threat as he gestured to the other men and they all fell back, although they stayed alert.

'I should go,' said Lotty.

She ruffled Pookie's fluffy head and put him on the ground. 'Be a good d-dog,' she told him, and Corran could hear the crack in her voice.

Biting her lip, Lotty stroked Meg's head and then raised her eyes to Corran's at last. 'I'll never forget my time here,' she said.

There was a great weight in his chest, pressing, pressing against his heart, holding him immobile. Unable to speak, Corran managed a stiff nod.

Lotty inhaled slowly, steadying herself, and then she turned and walked towards the helicopter.

Oblivious to the atmosphere, Pookie romped after her, head cocked eagerly as he looked up at her in expectation. Lotty stopped, and Pookie stopped too, his absurd tail wagging.

Corran found his voice. 'Pookie!'

Pookie glanced back at him, puzzled, but evidently decided that his place was with Lotty. In the end, Lotty picked up the little dog and carried him back to Corran. When she put Pookie in his arms, Corran saw that her eyes were swimming with tears, and his heart clenched painfully.

He thought about how hard she'd worked, about the difference she had made.

He thought about the feel of her, about turning to her in the night and finding her warm and soft and responsive.

He thought about how much he was going to miss her.

He thought about how much he loved her, and how he'd left it too late to tell her.

Now Pookie was whining in his arms and she was walking away once more.

'Lotty—' he called impulsively.

She paused, half turned so that she could look at him over her shoulder.

There ought to be some way to tell her how he felt, but Corran's mind went blank. All he could think was that she was leaving, and there was nothing he could do about it. 'Thank you,' was all he said in the end. 'Thank you for everything.'

Lotty looked at him for a moment, and she jerked her head, just as he had done when he had been unable to speak. Then she turned and walked on to the helicopter, her back very straight. An officer saluted, and they stooped to avoid the whirling propeller blades as he escorted her to the door.

She climbed in without looking back.

The rest of the officers followed. The door was pulled shut, the spinning propeller picked up speed and the helicopter lifted into the air. It hung there, ungainly, for a moment, before veering round and heading off down the glen, its shadow skimming over the silver surface of the loch.

Corran watched it until it receded into a tiny speck and finally disappeared. The birds settled back into the trees, ruffling their feathers. Pookie sighed. Meg lay down and put her nose on her paws. Silence rolled down from the hillsides.

She was gone.

Lotty stood at the window of her apartment, looking out over the lake. It was a pretty scene, with sailing boats making the most of the autumn sunshine, and trees along the lakeside turning red and gold, but her heart still ached for the silver loch and the austere hills of Mhoraigh.

And for the man who belonged there.

Caro came to stand beside her. She touched

Lotty's arm gently. 'Have you told your grand-mother yet?'

'Not yet, no.' Lotty mustered a smile. 'She's not going to be happy.'

'It's more important that *you're* happy,' said Caro. 'Are you sure this is what you want?'

'Yes, I'm sure.' It was the only thing Lotty had been sure of since seeing the double line on the strip. 'I'm having this baby.'

'What about Corran?'

It had been such a relief when Philippe had brought Caro back to Montluce. Lotty was fiercely glad for their happiness together, even if it did make her own misery more apparent. Caro's pres-ence changed the whole atmosphere in the palace. There was laughter in the long corridors and even the Dowager Blanche was seen to smile occasion-ally.

Reluctant to intrude on Caro's joy, Lotty kept her grandmother company, and took up her duties once more. Eventually she hoped to be able to pass them on to Caro, but for now Caro was busy planning a wedding at the beginning of December and at least visiting factories and schools and hospitals made Lotty fix on a smile and hold her head up.

So she smiled and shook hands, moving through the days on automatic pilot, but inside she felt as if she was blundering through a smothering fog of despair. She missed Corran desperately. At night she lay awake, aching for him, remembering him. If she thought about him hard enough, would he feel her? Would he pause and look up from whatever he was doing, sensing that she was dreaming of him?

Everyone in Montluce was treating her very gently, as if she had been through some traumatic experience. Nobody asked her what she had been doing, or why she had disappeared.

Only Caro wanted to know about her time at Loch Mhoraigh. Only Caro knew about Corran, and it was to Caro that Lotty went when the consequences of that reckless afternoon in the cottage bathroom, with the sun streaming through the window and the sawdust on the floor, finally caught up with her.

Blurry with unhappiness, it had taken her longer than it should have done to notice the signs of change in her body, and now she put a wondering hand on her stomach. It was an extraordinarily powerful feeling to know that a child was growing inside her.

Except that it wasn't extraordinary at all, really. Ordinary women around the world were having babies, just like her, and perhaps some of them were feeling the same jumbled mix of joy and terror and breathless awe at the miracle of it.

Caro was watching her in concern. 'Corran's going to be a father, Lotty. You have to tell him.'

'I know, and I will tell him, of course I will, but I can't yet, Caro.'

'Why not?'

Lotty hugged her arms together as she turned from the window. 'His ex-wife tricked him into marriage by pretending that she was pregnant. I'm not going to do the same thing.'

'You're not pretending,' said Caro, exasperated. 'You *are* pregnant!'

'But how will Corran know that?' asked Lotty. 'I spent two and a half months pretending to be someone else. Why should he believe me now?'

'If he loves you, he'll believe you.'

'He never said he loved me, Caro.' Lotty sank into a chair and pushed her hair back from her face. Her bob had nearly grown back in, and it was smooth and dark, just as it had always been. She looked almost like her old self.

She just felt different.

'Corran was very clear,' she told Caro. 'He's not ready for children yet. A disaster was the word he used. He's got too much to do getting the estate back on its feet. I'm not going to push him into a relationship he doesn't want. If I tell him about the baby now, of course he'll take responsibility. He'll say we should get married, just like he did to Ella, and saddle himself with the wrong kind of wife all over again.'

'You love him,' said Caro. 'Doesn't that make you the right kind of wife?'

'Not in Corran's book. He's determined to marry someone sensible and practical next time round, and I understand that. I think that's what he needs too.'

'You're sensible,' Caro insisted. 'You're practical too. Didn't you tell me you did all that cleaning and painting? How much more practical does he want?'

'He wants someone who'll belong,' said Lotty. 'Someone who's used to the isolation. Who can help with lambing if necessary, and who knows about farming and growing vegetables. Not someone like me, who didn't even know how to peel a potato.'

'You learnt, didn't you? Just like I had to learn how to behave in a palace.'

In spite of herself, a smile trembled on Lotty's lips. 'I saw you and Philippe laughing at the Ambassador's reception the other night. I'm sure that's not how you're supposed to behave!'

'That was Philippe's fault!' Caro grinned then sobered. 'The point is that I didn't belong here either, but I'm learning. It could be the same for you at Loch Mhoraigh. And don't you think Corran deserves to know he's going to be a father?'

'Of course he does, but not yet, Caro.' The arguments had been going round and round in Lotty's head until she was dizzy. 'I don't want Corran to feel as if he's being forced into anything. I don't want to be with him if that's how he feels.'

She saw that Caro was still looking dubious. 'When I've had the baby and am settled, I'll tell him then, I promise. I've got to tell Grandmère first, and the Crown Prince. They're going to be so disappointed. Perfect princesses aren't supposed to get pregnant!' she said with a twisted smile.

'Oh, Lotty!' Caro put her hand over Lotty's. 'What are you going to do?'

'I'm going to have this baby,' said Lotty. 'I know my grandmother won't like me being a single mother, and maybe the people won't like it either, but I've spent my whole life doing what everybody else expects of me.'

Her heart clenched at the thought of Corran, but she had meant what she told Caro. She would rather be by herself than push Corran into another disastrous marriage. Her time at Loch Mhoraigh had taught her that she was capable of doing whatever she set her mind to. She could be as strong as Raoul the Wolf when she needed to be. Wasn't that what she had wanted to learn when she ran away from Montluce?

'This is something I'm doing for myself, and for my baby,' she told Caro. 'I'm going to do it alone.'

CHAPTER TEN

'A pint of milk, please, and I'll take a packet of those biscuits.'

Corran avoided Mrs McPherson's eyes. He preferred to shop in the anonymity of the Fort William supermarket, but whenever he decided to drive past the village he'd remember Lotty telling him they should support the local shop. So then he would have to come in, like now, and listen to Betty talking about Lotty, whose progress she was following in the glossy magazines she loved.

The news that they had entertained a princess had riveted Mhoraigh, although there were plenty, like Betty McPherson, who claimed that they had always known there was something special about her.

Corran had known there was something special about Lotty too. He just hadn't realised that it involved a crown.

Everyone in Mhoraigh had hated him once; now

they pitied him. He was the frog who'd blown his chance with the princess.

Betty McPherson was very kind and often cooked him a meal to take home, but Corran hated the sympathy in her eyes. He hated the way she told him about the parties Lotty had been seen at, about the beautiful dresses she had worn. He hated the way he would drive back to the empty house afterwards and find that Lotty wasn't there.

She wasn't in the kitchen. She wasn't in the cottages, her hair tied up in that scarf, humming tunelessly as she painted. She wasn't walking Pookie down by the loch or sitting on the beach, sipping tea from the flask. She wasn't there when he reached for her in the night.

She was in Montluce, being a princess, and far, far out of his reach.

Corran had thrown himself into work on the estate, but nothing was the same any more. Pookie was forlorn, and even Meg looked reproachful. 'It's all for the best,' he found himself telling them as if they could understand him, but the words sounded hollow, even to himself.

And yet, how could it *not* be for the best? If Betty McPherson was to be believed, Lotty had slotted right back into her life in Montluce. It was absurd to hope that she might be missing Loch Mhoraigh, where there were no parties, no people, nowhere to wear those elegant clothes, and where her beauty was wasted on the hills and his mother's ridiculous little dog. And him.

She had been happy there, yes. Corran knew that. He remembered the way her eyes used to shine—but he remembered, too, that she had never once said that she wanted to stay for ever.

Why would she? Just once, Corran had given in to temptation and looked Princess Charlotte of Montluce up on the internet, and there she was. A fist had closed around his heart at the sight of her. She was the perfect princess, just as she'd told him. Corran read about her life, and how much everyone loved her. Not a single scurrilous story was attached to her. She was just very beautiful, very good, very royal.

Oh, and very rich.

What could a man like him, a working farmer struggling to restore an isolated, dilapidated estate, possibly have to offer Princess Charlotte of Montluce?

Betty McPherson rang up the milk and the

biscuits while Corran looked out at the first real snow of the season spitting from a leaden sky. He should stock up in case the track was ever impassable. Those were the kind of practicalities he should be thinking about, not how very far away Lotty seemed.

He opened his mouth to tell Betty that he would take more milk when she got in first. 'Have you seen our lassie's in the magazines again?'

Corran set his teeth. 'No,' he said. 'Betty, I think I might—'

'Look.' Ignoring him, she pulled a copy of *Glitz* from the top of the pile on the counter. *A Royal Rush Into Marriage!* was splashed across the cover over a picture of Prince Philippe and Lotty's friend, Caro. *Philippe and Caro Wed This Weekend.*

'Very nice,' said Corran. 'Could I have—'

'And here's our lassie.' Betty folded the page back and showed it to Corran. 'She looks peaky, doesn't she?' Her sharp blue eyes rested on Corran's face.

Corran didn't answer. He'd forgotten about milk and bread. He was staring down at the picture of Lotty. She looked strained, but beautiful still, standing next to some chinless wonder in a dinner jacket. Charlotte and Kristof: *Another Wedding in the Offing?*

There was another picture of Lotty on her own. The caption to that one read, *Charlotte's Bump: Could She be Pregnant?*

He picked up the magazine with hands that weren't quite steady and looked more closely at Lotty's stomach. It did look like a bump. Was it possible? But how long before a pregnancy showed? It was three and a half long, long months since Lotty had left.

Corran did the sums in his head and stiffened. Crushing the magazine in his hand, he stood for a moment staring unseeingly ahead of him before he turned on his heel and stalked out of the shop without thinking to pay for the magazine, or remembering the milk and biscuits left abandoned on the counter.

Betty McPherson smiled gently and put them back on the shelf.

The palace was alight with excitement. Lights blazed in the windows and the staterooms were filled with a hubbub of conversation as representatives from every part of Montluce mingled with the glamorous guests and visiting royalty who had been invited to see Prince Philippe marry Miss Caroline Cartwright the next day.

It was a long time since Montluce had seen a royal wedding, and the country was making the most of it. In spite of the snow, huge crowds had gathered outside the palace to ooh and aah at the guests as they arrived, and many had staked their claim on the roadside to watch the procession the next morning.

Lotty was working her way round the room, trying to talk to as many people as possible. She had pulled out all the stops to celebrate Caro and Philippe's wedding and was looking regal in a ball gown made of heavy Italian red silk. Her shoulders were bare except for the ancestral ruby and diamond necklace and she wore a tiara in her dark hair. The beautiful cut of the dress had been specially designed to draw attention away from her bump, but she had draped a chiffon stole over her arms as a further distraction.

Lotty wasn't ashamed of her pregnancy, but this party was in honour of Caro and Philippe and she didn't want anything to attract attention away from them tonight. Already there had been some speculation in the papers. Most of the reception guests were too polite to stare directly at her stomach, but Lotty could tell that they were wondering if the gossip was true or not.

So she smiled and chatted and hoped that nobody could see how tired she felt.

Standing up to her grandmother's fearsome will had been harder than Lotty had imagined. The Dowager Blanche had been devastated by Lotty's pregnancy and was unable to comprehend how she could even contemplate having the baby on her own. Her latest plan was to marry Lotty off to Count Kristof of Fleitenstien.

'He would raise the child as his own,' she assured Lotty. 'He understands how these things are done.'

Lotty didn't want *things done*. The baby was hers and Corran's. She wasn't going to pretend anything else. She wasn't going to pretend to love anyone she didn't. She had had enough of pretending.

Across the room, Lotty watched Caro and Philippe circulating amongst their guests. She was so happy for them, but whenever she saw the easy way they touched each other, the way they caught each other's eye in a moment of private amusement, she felt so lonely she could hardly breathe.

She missed Corran so much. She ached for him, hungered for him, like now, when the longing to be back at Loch Mhoraigh, pressed against him, was like a great hand closing around her throat. Sucking in her breath at the pain, Lotty closed her eyes without thinking.

'*Altesse?* Can I get you anything?'

Lotty's eyes snapped open and she fixed a smile automatically back into place. 'No, thank you. I'm fine.' From somewhere she summoned a name and set out to charm, but all the time she was remembering how different it had been with Corran, who never minced his words, who was caustic and abrupt and treated her exactly the way he treated everyone else.

Her gaze fixed courteously on the guest's face, she didn't at first register the commotion at the door, but as his gaze widened at something over her shoulder, she turned.

And froze.

There, pushing his way through the footmen, was Corran.

Corran, unmistakable, even in a dinner jacket and bow tie. Corran, grim-faced, looking tall and forbidding and utterly out of place under the glittering chandeliers in spite of his clothes.

Lotty stared, paralysed by shock, disbelief and incredulous, astounded joy.

He was striding across the ballroom, shaking off the footmen who hurried after him, searching the throng of guests with his eyes.

Looking for her.

Then he saw her. Even through the crowds, she could see the blaze of expression in his pale eyes as he checked, and headed straight for her. At the same time, security officers were converging on him from all sides, muttering hastily into the radios on their wrists, while the startled guests fell silent around them.

Lotty pulled herself together. She had to stop things before they got out of hand. They couldn't have a major security issue in the middle of Caro and Philippe's party.

Stepping forward, she gestured the security officers back before they could wrestle Corran to the ground, and he strode the last few yards unmolested until he stood right in front of her.

'There you are,' he said.

There was a rushing in Lotty's head and her vision darkened as a great tumble of emotions crashed through her. She didn't know whether to throw herself into Corran's arms or beat at his chest in fury. She was spinning wildly in a turmoil of anger and ecstasy and confusion and, leaping through it all, the astounding, wonderful knowledge that it was him, it was really him, he was there and nothing else mattered.

She couldn't faint. Lotty gripped the edges of her stole so tightly that her knuckles showed white. This was Caro and Philippe's party. She couldn't spoil it by making an exhibition of herself. Already half the room seemed to be turning to stare and a space was forming around them.

From somewhere Lotty found her princess smile and pinned it on.

'What are you doing here?' she asked through stiff lips.

'Is it true?' Corran demanded fiercely.

She knew what he meant, of course she did, but couldn't answer, not here in front of everyone. 'We can't talk about this now,' she said with an edge of desperation, and then, to her relief, Caro and Philippe were there, supporting her, looking from her to Corran and back again.

'Is everything all right?' Philippe rarely put on airs, but he could be daunting when he wanted to be.

'Yes,' said Lotty automatically.

Just as Corran snarled, 'No.'

He took hold of Lotty by the wrist. 'No, it's not all right,' he told Philippe flatly. 'I don't want to break up the party, but Lotty and I are going somewhere we can talk.'

Philippe took a protective step forward, but Caro had been watching Lotty's face and she put out a hand to hold him back. 'I think this must be Corran,' she said with a faint smile. 'I'm glad you've come,' she said to Corran. 'I hoped you would.'

Lotty found her voice. 'Corran, this is—'

'We'll do introductions later,' he interrupted her. 'Right now, you and I are getting out of here.'

Keeping a firm hold of her wrist, he turned without a further word to Philippe and Caro and dragged her towards the doors but, before he could reach them, he was baulked again. This time it was the Dowager Blanche herself who stepped into his way.

Lotty's grandmother was small and elderly, but she had a presence that could stop even Corran in his tracks. More than one person watching flinched at the expression on her face as she fixed Corran with gimlet eyes. She was, Lotty thought, far more frightening than the security officers on either side of her who were sliding their hands to their shoulder holsters.

'Take your hands off my granddaughter,' she said in freezing accents. 'Do you know who she is?'

Corran had stopped, but he didn't let Lotty go. 'I do,' he said, looking the Dowager Blanche right in the eyes. 'Do you?'

'This is Her Serene Highness Princess Charlotte!'

'No,' said Corran. 'This is Lotty.'

Lotty sucked in a breath and tried to interrupt before her grandmother annihilated him. 'Grandmère...' she began, but it was too late.

'How dare you speak to me like that?' Her grandmother's voice was like a lash. 'And how dare you talk about my granddaughter in that vulgar way?'

'I dare because I know her better than you do,' said Corran.

'You are impertinent!'

'I'm also right,' he said. 'I bet you don't know how out of tune she is when she hums or how she sticks her tongue out of the corner of her mouth when she's concentrating. Do you know how stubborn she is, how hard she works? How she stretches when she's tired, how grouchy she gets when her scones don't turn out? Do you know the *exact* angle she puts her chin in the air when she's crossed?

'I didn't think so,' said Corran when the Dowager looked astounded. 'Well, I do. I know the Lotty you'll never know. The Lotty who's fussy about her coffee and snappy if I forget to wipe my boots. Who smiles when she washes up and who hates cleaning her paintbrushes.'

His eyes went to Lotty and the two of them might as well have been alone, although all pretence at conversation had died around them and the entire ballroom was listening.

'The Lotty who's sweet and true and funny, who

made me happy and who left me all alone because I was too stupid to tell her how I felt.'

He turned back to the Dowager and his face hardened. 'You only know the princess. I know the woman. I may not know Princess Charlotte, but I know *Lotty.*'

His eyes flickered to the bodyguards. 'Now, I'd like to talk to her alone so I'd be glad if you'd call off your goons and let us leave.'

There was a frozen moment when the air between Corran and the Dowager fairly crackled and then, to Lotty's utter astonishment, her grandmother stood aside without another word.

'Thank you,' said Corran in a cool voice.

There was utter silence in the ballroom as he pulled Lotty out of the main doors to where the great state staircase swept down two sides to the marble hall. The area outside the doors was thronging with footmen and guests who had missed all the excitement. Corran ignored them all.

'God, how do we get out of here?'

Lotty found her voice at last. 'I'm not sure I want to go anywhere with you after embarrassing me like that.'

'You'll never be the perfect princess again,' Corran agreed. 'Your reputation's shot. There'll always be gossip about you now—and there'll be even more if we have our discussion here in front of everyone. I don't mind,' he said, 'but you might want some privacy.'

Lotty pressed her lips together, but she knew he was right. 'We'll go to my apartments,' she said.

An astonished footman sprang to life to throw open the door of the apartment for them. Head held high, Lotty swept in first.

Corran shut the footman out and turned to face Lotty, who was standing in the middle of a sumptuously decorated apartment. The diamonds in her tiara flashed in the light. Her head was high, her eyes bright with anger, and in the red ball gown she looked very much a princess.

'I don't appreciate being humiliated in front of my family, our staff and a ballroom full of guests,' she said icily.

'And I don't appreciate finding out from Betty McPherson that I'm a father!' Corran snapped back. 'How humiliating do you think *that* was?'

Lotty stared at him for a moment, and then she

dropped abruptly onto one of the sofas and covered her face with her hands.

'I'm sorry,' she said, her voice muffled. 'I'm so sorry, Corran.'

The anger leaked out of the air and Corran sat down heavily beside her. Gently, he pulled her hands from her face so that he could look into her eyes.

'It's true, then? You're having a baby?' His throat was very tight. 'Our baby?'

'Yes, it's true,' said Lotty, her fingers curling around his in spite of herself.

'It was that afternoon when we couldn't wait to go back to the house, wasn't it?' said Corran, and her cheeks warmed at the memory of the heat that had consumed them as the dust drifted in the sunlight and the smell of wood shavings filled the air.

'I think it must have been.'

'Why didn't you *tell* me, Lotty?'

She pulled her hands from his. 'You told me you weren't ready for children,' she reminded him. 'You told me how Ella tricked you into marriage by claiming to be pregnant. You told me you were never making a mistake like that again.' She swallowed.

'I didn't want to be a mistake, Corran,' she said, 'and I didn't want you to think of our baby as one. I was afraid that if I told you before the baby was born, you'd do exactly what you've done, and come rushing out to do your duty.'

'Duty?' said Corran slowly. 'Is that what you think this is?'

'What else can it be?' Lotty hugged her arms together to stop herself from reaching for him. 'I know how you feel. I know that the estate is your priority now. You think having a child would be a disaster, and you don't want to be stuck with a wife like me. I *know* all that.

'I don't blame you,' she went on quickly as Corran opened his mouth. 'I completely understand the kind of woman you need at Loch Mhoraigh.'

'Do you?' He put his head on one side and regarded her thoughtfully, a smile hovering for the first time around his mouth and in the depths of his eyes. 'What kind of woman is that?'

'You want a farmer's wife.' Her voice was dull and she fiddled with the ends of her stole. 'You need someone practical who's used to country living. I understand that.'

Corran nodded. 'I thought I needed a sensible, practical wife too. In fact, I was sure of it, but it turns out that what I *really* need is a princess who can't cook.'

Lotty leapt to her feet in agitation before he could go any further. 'You're just asking me because of the baby,' she said, wrapping her arms miserably around herself. 'I *knew* this would happen! That's why I didn't tell you.'

She took a turn around the room while she tried to get her thoughts in order. 'I don't need you to look after me, Corran,' she said eventually. 'I'm not denying you your rights as a father. I know you'll be a good one. I can see you don't want your child growing up split between two parents the way you did, but you'd never be like your father. I know Mhoraigh will be an important part of our child's life.

'I'll be fine on my own,' she said, lifting her chin in the unconscious gesture Corran recognised so well. 'I may be about to fall off my pedestal as far as the country is concerned, and my grandmother may be disappointed, but nobody's going to cast me out onto the street. Even if they were, I'd rather do that than know you were marrying me because you feel responsible.'

She'd done a full circuit and was back where she'd started. Corran was still sitting on the sofa, watching her with an unreadable expression.

'You'd feel trapped and resentful, and that's no way to start a marriage,' she told him. 'You've already been through that once, and I'm not going to do that to you again.'

'Finished?' said Corran, getting to his feet in his turn.

Lotty's eyes flickered around the room as she tried to work out if that was a trick question or not.

'Yes,' she said, but doubtfully.

'Good, so perhaps I can have my say now?'

'All right,' she said with a wary look.

Corran took a deep breath. 'I know you don't need me, Lotty,' he said. 'Why do you think it's taken me so long to come and find you? Look at you,' he went on, gesturing at the diamonds around her neck, the tiara in her hair. 'You're a *princess!* You live in a palace! You've got everything you could ever want. What can a man like me possibly give you that you don't already have?

'You don't need me, Lotty,' he said again, 'but *I* need *you*. I need you desperately. I thought that all I needed was Loch Mhoraigh. I thought if I could be where I belonged, I'd be fine, but I've learnt that belonging is about people as much as about place. You taught me that,' he told her. 'You made me realise that Loch Mhoraigh is just a place, and that I'll belong anywhere as long as I'm with you.'

'But the baby…?' she managed.

'The baby gave me the courage to come and tell you myself,' said Corran. 'I'd been sitting there at Loch Mhoraigh, missing you, wishing I'd told you how much I loved you before you left. Furious with myself for not asking you to stay while I had the chance.'

He took hold of the ends of her stole and used it to draw Lotty towards him, very slowly. 'Whenever I went into the shop, Betty McPherson would tell me how she'd been reading about you in the magazines and it sounded as if you were having a wonderful time, going to parties and doing all the things you never did at Loch Mhoraigh. I thought you were happy,' he said.

Lotty shook her head slowly. 'I wasn't happy.'

'Then Betty showed me the picture where they were speculating about you being pregnant, and you looked sad. You didn't look the way you looked at Loch Mhoraigh, and then I thought, what if she isn't happy? What if it's not too late to tell her that I love her? What if she really is having my baby, and needs me now even a fraction of the way I need her? I knew how hard it would be for you. I couldn't bear the thought of you dealing with your grandmother and the press and everyone else all on your own when I ought to be with you. I was furious with myself for not being with you, and furious with you for not telling me.

'And so I came,' he said simply. 'I didn't stop to think about what I would say when I got here. I heard about the party tonight and I knew you'd be there. I've got mates who work as bodyguards so I know how these things work—and, by the way, your security team isn't quite as tight as it ought to be! There's no way I should have been able to get to you.

'But I did, and there you were, standing in the

middle of the floor, and you looked so beautiful, like the princess you are, but you were *you* too…'

Corran broke off, looking ruefully down into Lotty's face. 'Sorry, I'm not explaining this very well, am I? It was just…when I looked into your eyes, I didn't see Princess Charlotte. I saw Lotty— the Lotty I've missed so desperately since you left. The Lotty I belong with.'

'Oh, Corran…' Lotty's mouth trembled and Corran let go of the stole to take her hands instead.

'Everything I told your grandmother—and all those people who were listening, agog—is true. I'm not in love with Princess Charlotte, but I *am* in love with you. Please tell me you've missed me too, Lotty. Tell me you need me and love me, even if it's just a little bit.'

'Oh, Corran, of course I do!' Her voice broke. 'Of course I love you!'

Lotty's tears spilled over as he pulled her hard against him and his arms closed around her at last. She buried her face into his throat and wept while he held her and murmured endearments into her hair. 'I'm just so happy and I've been so lonely without you,' she sobbed.

'You don't sound very happy,' said Corran and she gave a watery laugh and lifted her face at that.

'I am,' she promised, winding her arms around his neck. 'I *am*.'

They kissed, almost tentatively at first as if they could hardly believe that they were really there, touching at last. It felt so good to be kissing Corran again, to be holding him tight. Lotty pressed against his lean, hard body and would have wept again at the pleasure and the piercing relief of it if she had had the breath to spare, but the sweetness of the kiss was spinning her round and round until she was dizzy and dazed with happiness.

'Are you sure?' she mumbled between kisses as they broke for breath. 'I don't want to get married just because it's the right thing to do.'

Corran was backing her over to the sofa, easing her down onto the cushions without once taking his warm lips from her throat. 'It's up to you,' he said as he kissed his way along her jaw. 'If you're determined to ruin your reputation as the perfect princess, we'll live in sin and you can thumb your nose at the press. As long as we're together, I don't mind.'

He rested his hand on her stomach and lifted his head to smile down at her. 'But I think we might as well get married, don't you? I'll make sure our children know that they have a wild and wicked princess for a mother and you can pretend to be unconventional!'

Lotty laughed, but made a face. 'I think I've done enough pretending,' she said. 'Have you forgiven me yet?'

'I will if you'll come back to Loch Mhoraigh with me.'

'Oh, I'd love to do that,' sighed Lotty.

Corran sat up, pulling her with him. 'Why do I get a feeling there's a *but* coming up? Do you need to stay in Montluce?'

'No. From tomorrow, Caro will be Montluce's princess, and I can step back. I wasn't thinking about my duties here,' Lotty told him. Drawing a deep breath, she tried to sit back, but Corran kept both arms firmly around her. 'Montluce isn't the problem; I am,' she said. 'The truth is that I'm not the right kind of wife for you, Corran. You *do* need someone useful, and I'm not.'

'I disagree,' said Corran, smoothing her hair back from her face. 'You may not be the best cook in the world, but you've got very useful social skills. If it wasn't for you dragging me to that ceilidh and charming everyone there, I would still be cut off from the village. As it is, I've been inundated with casseroles and cakes from Betty McPherson and everyone else in the village who feels sorry for me for being stupid enough to let you go. And you impressed Dick Rowland enough for him to invest in the estate. That's much more useful than being able to drive a tractor or help with the lambing.'

Lotty sat up a little straighter. 'I suppose that's true. And we know I can clean and paint.'

'No more hard labour for you until after the baby is born,' he said firmly. 'You can just concentrate on making me happy. That's where you're really useful.'

'Oh, well, if I must,' she said, smiling, and winding her arms around his neck as he kissed her again.

Some time later, she heaved a blissful sigh and rested her head against Corran's shoulder. 'I'm Caro's bridesmaid, so we'll have to stay until after the wedding tomorrow, but then we can go home. I can't wait!' Smiling, she pulled off her tiara and let it dangle from her fingers. 'I won't be a princess any more.'

'You'll always be a princess,' said Corran, taking the tiara and putting it back on her head. 'But you'll always be Lotty too, and you'll be a wife, and you'll be a mother. You'll be *yourself*.'

'No more pretending,' she realised.

'No more pretence,' he agreed. 'For either of us. We'll be true to ourselves and true to each other, and we'll love each other and we'll be together. What more do we need?'

Twining her fingers with his, Lotty leant in for another long, sweet kiss and thought about going home with him. She thought about the big grey house waiting for her by the water, about the hills and the cool, clean air.

And she thought about Corran, about the man he was and the life they would share, and the child they would love.

'Nothing,' she said.

* * * * *

Mills & Boon® Large Print
January 2012

THE KANELLIS SCANDAL
Michelle Reid

MONARCH OF THE SANDS
Sharon Kendrick

ONE NIGHT IN THE ORIENT
Robyn Donald

HIS POOR LITTLE RICH GIRL
Melanie Milburne

FROM DAREDEVIL TO DEVOTED DADDY
Barbara McMahon

LITTLE COWGIRL NEEDS A MUM
Patricia Thayer

TO WED A RANCHER
Myrna Mackenzie

THE SECRET PRINCESS
Jessica Hart

1211 Rom LP

Mills & Boon® Large Print

February 2012

THE MOST COVETED PRIZE
Penny Jordan

THE COSTARELLA CONQUEST
Emma Darcy

THE NIGHT THAT CHANGED EVERYTHING
Anne McAllister

CRAVING THE FORBIDDEN
India Grey

HER ITALIAN SOLDIER
Rebecca Winters

THE LONESOME RANCHER
Patricia Thayer

NIKKI AND THE LONE WOLF
Marion Lennox

MARDIE AND THE CITY SURGEON
Marion Lennox